Matthews, J
PICTURES OF THE
JOURNEY BACK

COP 1

JUL 2 '73 BEALE			

Pictures of the Journey Back

Other books by Jack Matthews

Pictures of the Journey Back

by Jack Matthews

Harcourt Brace Jovanovich, Inc. • *New York*

**For Sam
and all my good friends
in Kansas**

I owe special thanks to Ohio University for a sabbatical leave in 1970–1971 which gave me time to write this novel.

First edition
ISBN 0–15–171920–9
Library of Congress Catalog Card Number: 72–88802
Printed in the United States of America
B C D E

Pictures of the Journey Back

1 The Skelly service station is one mile south of Zimmerdale, on the west side of Route 81, going straight down to Wichita. The bright Skelly sign shines forth like an emblem of civilization in the darkness of this November dawn. To the east, between the vaguely rising sun and the oasis of light that is this gasoline station upon a Kansas highway, lie the atavistic Flint Hills, rolling prairie land covered with buffalo grass and approximately one snarled thorn tree per thousand acres. The sight of this land in late autumn would blight the eyes of a vulture, someone once said; but no one heard him, and the hawks don't give a damn anyway.

Now, the cold dawn wind blows hard and tirelessly past the gas pumps, rattling the dozen signs announcing tire and lube specials, and making the windows drum in their sashes.

The station has been open only half an hour, serving three customers in the first fifteen minutes, and none in the second. Inside the station, the manager and his young assistant read separate sections of the Wichita *Eagle*. The manager pauses now and then to sip at a Dixie Cup filled with sugared black coffee. His assistant occasionally drinks from a Dr Pepper bottle, making a loud pop from the suction of his mouth every time he takes the bottle away. Outside, the wind beats, drums, blasts, whirs, and fumbles at the building, not disturbing the warm peacefulness inside. On the back wall, a clock ticks steadily, indifferent to the impetuous assaults of the wind.

At two minutes after seven, there is a heavy bang to the rear, and the assistant sets his Dr Pepper down and says, "That the women's room again?"

"Sounds like it. Did you unlock it?"

"I always unlock it in the morning," the assistant says, tossing his paper aside and getting up. The banging sound is repeated several times, slightly diminished.

The assistant stretches, while the manager turns a page of

the newspaper and shakes it out before his eyes, like a man setting a painting straight.

The assistant goes out the front door and around to the women's room and pulls the door shut. Coming back, he leans forward into the wind, staring balefully at the leakage of cold sunlight glowing somewhere above and beyond the Flint Hills.

When he reaches for the front door, the light on his outstretched arm changes slightly, and he turns around to see a battered green 1969 Ford pickup, with the headlights still on, glide into the station. He hunches his shoulders into the wind and climbs out toward it. An old guy with the battered face of an ex-boxer gets out, hanging onto the door as if he intends to throw the whole truck in the direction of the office . . . but it's only the wind pulling against his arm, and he turns around and closes it. He's wearing a Stetson that looks as old and battered as the Ford, and when he starts trotting toward the office, holding the Stetson down with one hand and limping heavily, he calls out, speaking in a hoarse, heavy voice with an almost unnatural slowness: "Fill the damn thing up."

"Regular?" the attendant asks, turning around, but his voice is lost in the deafening wind whir, so he turns the crank on the regular pump, pulls off the cap to the tank, and shoves the nozzle in. Then he himself runs into the office.

". . . right outside of McPherson," the old cowboy is saying when the door goes shut.

"What's that?" the assistant asks.

The manager turns to him and says, "They's a semi blowed off the road right outside of McPherson."

"Damn," the assistant says. "Just now?"

"Just when I come past there," the cowboy explains in his heavy, slow voice. "The highway patrol was there, but it had just happened, you could tell. I mean, they was flares burning in the road and everything, but only this here one patrol car, and a couple of other cars. Right before the turnoff on 35."

"Wind blow it off?" the assistant asks.

"I don't know what else," the cowboy states, sounding faintly surprised at the question.

The assistant nods, and then says, "Did you say regular?"

"It don't make no damn difference with that old thing," the cowboy says. "Not the way I have beat it around through the years. By now, I have just about got her tamed."

"I mean, that wind is *cold!*" the assistant cries, shoving his hands in his pockets, shivering all over, and dancing on his toes.

The cowboy nods emphatically and looks out at his pickup. He takes a couple fingers of chewing tobacco and shoves it in his mouth.

"Sure is," the manager says in a devout voice. "I've lived in this country all my life, but there's one thing a man can never get used to, and that's the wind."

The cowboy nods abstractedly, but doesn't really seem to be listening.

"Want me to check under the hood?" the assistant asks.

Now he shakes his head no, and says, "I could probably use me some damn oil, but I'll let it go for now. I have got to get my ass moving on to Wichita."

The assistant nods and hunches his shoulders up, watching the dial turn on the face of the pump outside. He shivers, and nods again, even though no one has said anything. The manager has picked up his paper again, and sits there behind his desk reading it.

The cowboy says in his slow gruff voice: "Time waits for no damn man."

"That's the truth!" the assistant agrees, nodding faster.

The cowboy stamps his foot heavily, as if something is sticking to it, and says, "Damn leg freezes up on me like a *log* if I ride very long! Ever time."

The dial hand on the pump stops, and the assistant goes out and milks the last of the gas into the tank, puts the cap back on, and returns, jogging, to the office.

"Six thirty-two," he says, looking at the old cowboy's pocket.

The cowboy takes a wad out of his pocket and peels off a ten. The assistant gets out three one-dollar bills, two quarters, a dime, a nickel, and three pennies, and lays them silently in the cowboy's big open hand. When all the change is there, the cowboy pockets it, and opens the door into the wind.

"Hurry back," the manager says, turning the last page of the paper.

"Sure will," the cowboy says, without turning his head. He moves, leaning against the wind, toward the pickup, holding tight to his Stetson. Beyond him, the eastern sky is a little brighter, but the wind is still cold with the night and seems to carry blackness with it, smudging the lights that shine upon the cement apron before them.

A ragged piece of old newspaper, blown out of nowhere, is suddenly pasted against the cowboy's leg, and he leans over a little—stiff in the back—and peels it slowly off his knee and thigh. He looks at it momentarily, still holding tight to his Stetson, as if he is about to read it; but then he lets it go, and it flaps wildly away into the void.

The assistant watches all of this; and then watches as the cowboy slowly climbs up out of the wind into the pickup, starts the engine, and commences driving south once more on 81 toward Wichita.

2 Somewhere in the northeast section of the city, near the university, J. Dan Swope eases his Ford pickup over to the curb and looks up at the house. It is an ugly little place: a single-story, gray-shingled, box-shaped thing, hooded on all sides by an overhanging roof that lies in flat triangles up to the peak at the center. A wide-spreading oak tree squats in the front yard like something carved from dark creaking granite, some of its leafless branches leaning heavily on the roof of the house. A bent aluminum TV antenna lies rusting on its shoulder in the scrawny hedge, one slack lead still hanging from the roof.

Tin numbers are nailed to the shingles by the front door: 653. J. Dan climbs out of the pickup, shakes his stiff leg, and then walks around in front. For a moment he stands there rubbing the back of his neck and looking at the house. This is sure as hell the address: 653 Fernway. He hesitates for an instant, as if his mere presence might evoke her from the house, but then he shoves his hands down in his pockets and starts up the front walk to the door. A sudden gust of wind rattles the limbs of the oak, and J. Dan hunches his shoulders deeper into the badly scratched and worn suede jacket he has been wearing for years. He doesn't take the trouble to button his jacket up, and he instinctively and accurately ducks his head to the side so that his old Stetson will blot out the chilly wind.

When his boots hit the front porch, the hollow sound they make suggests that the porch is beginning to rot. The whole house is full of termites, probably. The neighborhood itself looks nibbled and shabby, as a matter of fact. The yard next door is separated from this one by an old farm fence, scarcely strong enough to hold up the dead wild rose vines that are scrawled all over it, leafless and knotted with thorns.

J. Dan takes three steps across the porch and knocks heavily on the loose screen door. He turns around and faces the street again, looking at the pickup, wondering how the high gear is holding out, and wondering if it will get them there.

No one answers, so he turns and knocks again, this time louder and harder, making the door rattle angrily in its frame. Then he turns back to stare outwards—gazing over the pickup and over the little houses standing in the dead weeds across the street, and up at the pale-blue morning sky, so placid and still-looking in spite of the cold wind.

When no one answers, he lifts his hand and looks at his watch and sees that it is ten after nine. Maybe she works; but then, she didn't say anything about that in the letter she wrote to him.

J. Dan walks off the porch, and sees a woman coming out of the house next door. She is wearing slacks and a long coat with tattered sleeves, and she has a scarf wrapped sideways around her head.

When she glances in his direction, J. Dan starts toward her across the yard, and says, "I am wondering if there's a Laurel Burch who lives here."

"Is that the girl?" the woman asks.

"It might be. Is she here now?"

The woman stops and shoves both her hands in her overcoat pockets. "It's hard to tell," she says. "Neither one of them's there very much, I don't think. At least, I don't ever see much of them. I don't know where they are. Maybe they're still asleep. It's still early."

J. Dan nods and looks away, and the woman goes on out to the street and gets into a fairly new-looking blue Datsun.

J. Dan watches her drive away, and then turns around once again and looks at the house. "Neither one of them," he says half out loud, and with so many pauses that he almost sounds slow-witted. "Well, damned if I knew they was another one. I wonder if it's male or female."

He gets back in his truck and drives away, deciding he'll go get himself some breakfast, and then come back and pitch camp on the porch if he has to, until the brainless little puppy bitch returns.

3 A fat woman wiped off the counter in front of him and said, "What'll it be this morning?"

J. Dan frowned at the menu, and then held it out a little farther from his eyes.

"Didn't it get *cold* last night?" the woman said. "I hear it got down to twenty-three, and with that wind . . . I tell you, this is sure funny weather. It's supposed to get up to the low seventies today. Now you know, it just don't make sense to have the temperature go from twenty-three to seventy in twenty-four hours. I wouldn't be surprised if it turns out to be tornado weather. They say there might be some warnings out west of here, later on in the day."

J. Dan nodded and frowned harder at the menu. He was so tired and chilled, his damn eyes didn't seem to want to work right. For a minute he just sat there looking at the words, forgetting all about breakfast.

"Bacon and eggs?" the woman prompted. "With home fries on the side? And coffee?"

J. Dan looked at her, having forgotten how hungry he was, and nodded.

"*That* sounds good," the woman said, wiping her hands on a towel and walking away. Her tone was comfortable and a little maternal. J. Dan laid the menu down and closed his eyes for a moment.

"Want those eggs over?" the woman called back. "Or up?"

"Over," J. Dan said. He sighed and wiped his eyes with his hands, rubbing them until the skin got warm and began to tingle. Then he turned around on his stool and looked out through the window at the cold, sunny morning.

Twice the night before he'd stopped and tried to sleep, but the wind had chilled the cab in ten minutes, waking him up. Maybe Laurel had a place he could sleep for a while, before they started back. If she was back home yet. Or if *they* were, whoever the other one was.

Only they ought to get started back; there wasn't any time to waste. No damn time to sleep.

He turned around again and rested his forearms on the counter. His old battered gray Stetson was shoved back on his head, and when he glanced in the mirror behind the counter, back of the pie shelves, beyond the banana cream, peach, and

9

raisin, he could see his face: unshaven, wrinkle-eyed from both fatigue and years of squinting in the wind and sun, and looking sure as hell like death warmed over. Well, it was true; he'd never looked this old before; but then, the truth was, he'd never *been* this old before. He half dozed on the thought.

"Here's your eggs and bacon," the fat woman said, tidying the silverware beside the plate she set before him. "I'll get your toast in a minute. Wait a minute: didn't I bring you no coffee?"

J. Dan looked down before him and saw that she hadn't.

"Why *that* ain't no way to treat a man!" the woman cried, whipping around and pouring the coffee in a cup. "You like cream?" she asked over her shoulder.

J. Dan nodded and said yes, and when she set the cup of coffee and cream down, she said, "Now the sugar is right there, if you want it. Right there."

He looked and saw that it was. She must know that he was only about half awake, and dead tired, by the way she was treating him. She was a round-faced woman, with a pursed-up mouth, bright sassy eyes behind horn-rimmed glasses, and gray hair in a bun at the back of her head.

She was in her fifties, maybe: a middle-aged woman like you see just about everywhere, and don't even notice. J. Dan contemplated the fact that he was just damn near about the same vintage.

4 After breakfast, he drove back to 653 Fernway and parked in front. He took out his pouch of Redman and packed some in his mouth. It was about ten o'clock, and even though there didn't seem to be any cars on the street that hadn't been there before, he decided to go up and try the door again. And if she wasn't here this time, he'd have to get on over to the university and see if he could find her there and dig her out.

But after he knocked on the door, he heard, or felt, someone walking heavily inside the house. It was like someone half awake stumbling along in stockinged feet. And then the door trembled a little as it was unlocked, and opened just enough to show the head of a bearded boy. The boy stared at him an instant without speaking, and then in his slow voice J. Dan said, "I am looking for Laurel Burch."

The boy blinked as if he were sorting through a number of names, and then half nodded by merely lowering his face a few inches and leaving it there. The boy was slightly taller than J. Dan, and wide, but hollow-chested and flat. His face was long and bony, with thick blond sideburns, a long drooping mustache, and a haze of whiskers on the chin. Elsewhere, the beard was as indefinite as hairs on the arm or leg. His green eyes were intelligent and wide apart. He somewhat resembled a goat.

"Wait a minute," the boy said in a quick, hoarse tenor, and half closed the door. Then the door swung open a little farther than before, and the boy said, "I mean, who *is* it? Who's wanting her?"

"Just tell her that J. Dan is here. She'll know who it is: J. Dan Swope."

The boy stared at him, as if to question him further, but then he closed the door and disappeared. However, the door didn't close all the way, and a cold draft pushed it back far enough for J. Dan to hear the boy say, "Laurel, you better get up. Your mother's crazy old cowboy's at the door."

J. Dan turned around and walked to the edge of the porch and eased a gob of chewed and distilled Redman down past the step into the dead weeds of the flower bed. Then he stretched backward, took a deep breath, put his hands in his hip pockets and stared out at the street until he heard the squeak of the door opening a little. He turned around and looked at Laurel standing there in a long shabby brown robe, planted solidly on her naked feet.

"Well, this is sure as hell a surprise," she said. "I didn't think you'd come all the way here."

"Well, I did," J. Dan said.

"Even after I told you the answer was no," she said. She frowned, hugged herself and shivered. "Well, shit, come on in!"

J. Dan removed his Stetson and followed her solemnly into the house. The room was dark and dirty, with paperback books and photographs scattered all about . . . some on chairs and others on the floor. There was a fireplace for a gas burner, but it was cold and stuffed with dirty rags. Above the chipped wooden mantel was a large, life-sized photograph of a naked woman giving suck to a chimpanzee dressed in a tuxedo. The woman was wearing pince-nez glasses and a high, expensively coiffured wig.

A large sheet of gray art paper was Scotch-Taped to the wall at one side, and on it were pasted individual letters cut out from the slick paper of a magazine, looking like a ransom note and saying: GOD IS A WOMAN AND SHE HATES TO DO HOUSEWORK.

"Sit down," Laurel said vaguely. She didn't seem to be aware of the room at all. She scratched at the back of her head, momentarily closing her eyes.

Then she said, "Just throw that shit on the floor," and motioned vaguely toward the chair. "I'll go get some clothes on. You want some coffee? Or a glass of Rhine wine?"

"No," J. Dan stated, settling down in the room's only upholstered chair. "I have just got through having me some breakfast."

"Hey," she said, scratching her scalp again, "did you knock on the door about an hour ago?"

J. Dan nodded, and she said, "Jeffrey told me he heard someone at the door. Or thought he did. I didn't hear a thing. I mean, I simply disappear or like *evaporate* or something when I go to sleep."

"That's all right," J. Dan said. "I was ready to get me some damn breakfast anyway. An empty stomach makes a man grumpy."

"I mean, I'm really sorry you wasted your time coming all this way, J. Dan," she said. She pushed her fists down into the old robe so hard it opened up in front enough to show the cleavage between her breasts. J. Dan stared at her without answering. She must be quite a piece, her and her long legs, her big hips, slightly buck teeth, and big, jug-sized tits. And those big pretty eyes that could almost melt a belt buckle or pair of scissors. And that long pale dirty brown hair that hung down to her shoulders. Yes, she must be quite a piece, and a real tough broad underneath all that soft and innocent look.

"Well, it won't do you any good, but we can talk about it as soon as I put something on," she said, and left the room. J. Dan crossed one leg over the other and toyed with the brim of his Stetson, wondering what had happened to the bearded boy. Then he looked back at the large picture of the lady giving suck to the chimpanzee, and slowly and wonderingly shook his head back and forth.

"Hey, you want a glass of wine or something?" the boy asked, coming back into the room.

"No, I just had me some breakfast," J. Dan said.

The boy nodded and stood there with his hands hanging shallow in his Levi's, gazing distantly over J. Dan's head. Then he yawned, and rubbed the back of his neck with one hand, leaving his other one in his pocket.

"Wow!" he said, blinking his eyes. "Wow!"

J. Dan felt embarrassment for the poor nut, and looked away, drumming his fingers on the Stetson and trying to find something decent to look at. He settled for an aquarium near the front window, glowing and bubbling there in the room's darkness. He couldn't see any fish in it though, and this began to trouble him. He gazed at it for a couple of minutes, trying to see

13

if maybe some guppies, at least, or moonfish were hiding behind the thin strands of plant life, but he couldn't see anything move at all, except for the bubbles coming up regularly to the surface.

He looked back at the blown-up photograph of the naked woman and the chimp, and then back at the boy, who still stood there exactly as he had been before, his hands hanging loosely in his pockets and his gaze pointed distantly at the wall beyond J. Dan's head. He looked a little as if he might be hypnotized.

Eventually, Laurel came back, dressed like the boy, in Levi's and a grayish-white T-shirt. She didn't have a bra on, and her two tits bounced and wiggled with every step. She went to a wooden folding chair leaning against the wall, opened it, and placed it in the middle of the floor. It had "Greer's Funeral Home" stenciled in faded black paint on the back. Then she sat down on it, facing J. Dan, and said, "Well, let's get it over with: is she still alive?"

"Yes, she is still hanging on. I called the hospital the minute I come into Wichita, and they said there was no change. It's a miracle she is, but she's still alive."

Laurel nodded and then looked down at her thumbnail and started picking at something on it. The boy hadn't moved. J. Dan uncrossed his legs, and looked back at the photograph above the mantel.

"Look," Laurel said finally, without raising her eyes from her thumbnail, "I told you: I am not coming. That's all there is to it. There's nothing I can do, and there's absolutely no point in being like *hypocritical*. My proud, beautiful, eternally well-groomed, and disapproving mother and I haven't been able to communicate with each other for a long, long time, J. Dan, and there's no use pretending this late. And you know it."

"That don't have nothing to do with it," J. Dan said.

"Bullshit."

"She has got to see you one more time. Just once, and that

14

is it. Forever. And the obligation is done. And that is why I have come to get you. Right is right."

"I tell you, I'm not coming. I mean, I'm not like *obliged*. So why don't you just turn the fuck around and go back to her yourself."

"I aim to," J. Dan said, shaking his head. "With you sitting right there on the seat beside me."

"Listen, I'm not about to go through all that hypocritical shit and go back there and put on a big deathbed scene. Can't you understand that? For me to go back there now, after all that's passed between us, would be dishonest to my own feelings."

"I always figure people have a lot of different feelings," J. Dan said. "And I don't know why you just have to listen to some of them and not to the other ones."

Laurel gazed up at him a moment. The boy sneezed loudly into his hand, and then quickly sneezed again.

"*Gesundheit*," J. Dan said.

"Thanks," the boy said, and then he went over to the window behind J. Dan and moved the blind aside so he could see out. It was as if he were going there for a drink of light.

"What's all this to you?" Laurel said, standing up suddenly and raising her voice. "I mean, if you were my real father or something, or even *married* to her, I could understand all this moralistic and philosophic bit from my favorite cowshit Socrates. But just because you've been living with her all these years and balling her any goddam time you want, and giving her money and buying her expensive clothes so she could keep that precious, fucking hypocritical *pride* of hers . . . and letting her nurse you back from your hangovers . . . you think you've got some kind of proprietary right in the matter, and can come here all this way to take me back to the lovely old bitch just because she happens to be dying and never once gave a shit for me anyway, as a *person*, and—"

She stopped suddenly and sat back down, pulling her hair

into her face with both hands, and breathing rapidly into it.

"Now come on," J. Dan said. "There is no damn reason you have got to say things like that."

"Oh, shit!" she cried. "You just don't understand! You don't understand *anything*, and you never have! How could you?"

"Well, I don't think there is any reason you have got to act this way," J. Dan said. "If you would just come along with me like you ought to, why then there wouldn't be no *reason* to get so damn upset."

"Oh, *that's* not the reason," Laurel said, sniffing and frowning down at her thumbnail again.

Behind J. Dan, the boy said, "Hey, I mean, is that *your* pickup?"

J. Dan turned around and said, "What?"

"That pickup out there in front. Is that yours?"

"If it's a green '69 Ford half-ton pickup with dust all over her, and a snarled right fender, she is mine."

"Wow!" the boy said. "God, I've always dug those crazy things. I mean, ever since I was a kid. You know?"

J. Dan turned around once again and looked at the boy, who was still peering out the window, the blind half covering his head and shoulder. Laurel sniffed and said, "J. Dan, you don't know. I'm sorry to tell you this, but *you just don't know*."

"Don't know what?" J. Dan asked, turning back to face her.

She stood up and thrust her hands in her pockets and said, "J. Dan, if I could tell you that . . . oh, shit, forget it!"

"Well, then tell me so I'll know," J. Dan said. "A man can always learn, and I am ready."

"No."

"I am staying right here until you come with me," he said. "If you're worried about your classes at the university, I will explain it all to them. They are not going to try to keep you from seeing your dying mother, and you damn well know it."

"Oh, it isn't my classes, J. Dan. I'm not in school this term, anyway. I've dropped out. It's a drag."

16

"What's that say on the door?" the boy asked.

"It don't say nothing," J. Dan said slowly. "That's just some name I gave it one time."

"You gave it a *name?*"

"I guess I'm not the only one that ever done that," J. Dan said irritably. "No reason to go get so damn excited."

"I'm not excited, man; but, I mean, it's like naming a *horse!*"

J. Dan shifted uncomfortably and said, "Well, in a way, maybe it is. I have taken her through many a mile of range."

The boy was quiet an instant as he squinted through the window, trying to see the small print on the door of the pickup.

"What does it say? It looks like 'Betty Boop' or something."

"That's pretty near," J. Dan said, nodding. "She's called 'Betty Bump.'"

"Oh no!" the boy cried, spinning around from the window and collapsing against the wall. "That's too *much*, man!"

J. Dan turned around and looked at his alert, goatish face, and Laurel said, "Never mind him, J. Dan. Don't pay too close attention and you won't get so up tight."

"Too *much!*" the boy said, closing his eyes and scratching his stomach.

J. Dan looked back at Laurel a moment, turning his Stetson around in his hands. Then he nodded.

"How many miles you got on it?" the boy asked, his head once more behind the blind.

"Over ninety-three thousand," J. Dan said. "And Laurel here is going to see it turn on over to ninety-four thousand if the damn transmission holds out."

"I am not," Laurel said violently. "Absolutely *am fucking not!*"

"Wow!" the boy said, turning away from the window and letting the blind fall back with a clatter.

"No," Laurel said, "because I mean, whatever I do, I have to be honest with myself." A calico cat walked into the room then, and Laurel leaned over, picked it up and nestled it under her left breast. She kissed it and said, "Hello, Zarathustra."

"You don't have to pack much," J. Dan stated. "You don't even have to dress up."

"That's a laugh," she said, still looking at the cat.

"And I sure would appreciate it if you would hurry up and give in, because I am getting awful damned tired and sleepy. I drove all night. And I didn't hardly get no sleep last night, either."

"Stop it," she said. Then in her falsetto imitation of a senile old woman's voice that J. Dan had almost forgotten, she said, "You're breaking my heart when you talk like that!"

"Looks like it'd be hard to do that," J. Dan said, "with them big pretty sweet *meat* cushions you got protecting it."

Laurel looked at him for an instant, then dropped the cat on the floor and went to the mantel, where she got a pack of cigarettes and shook one out.

"I have got to take me a spit," J. Dan said. He got up, went out the front door stiff-legged, and spit over the railing of the porch. It was still cold, and the wind was still strong, blowing out of the northwest. He stared squinting into the wind for a few seconds and then turned around and went back into the house. He was surprised to see Laurel and the goat-faced boy standing face to face; the boy was talking in his low, rapid, hoarse voice to her, but J. Dan couldn't hear what he was saying. When he came back in, the boy stopped, and both Laurel and he looked at him.

"No," Laurel said, speaking slowly and with exaggerated distinctness, to some indeterminate space between them. "No, I simply do not *want* to!"

"But I mean this is too much to pass by," the boy said in a half-whisper. "It's like a gift, you know?"

"No, I don't," Laurel said, not looking at him. "No, no, *no!* I'm trying to figure out what's fucking my head up, and here you are—"

18

"I've already started it, and it's like this is the second movement. What the first was waiting for."

"You're talking shit again," Laurel said in a tired, disappointed voice.

"Look, we've *got* to go. I can't explain it all now, but I know it's got to be. Look at it this way: I'll be with you. It isn't going to be all that bad with me along. And I mean, you can take your notebook along and work on poems. You know, with the land drifting by outside. It's like living in a river of images. It'll shake you loose and bring you like *together* again! It's stupendous! I mean, for *both* of us!"

Laurel frowned dramatically, ran her hand through her hair and said, "Oh, shit!" Then she put the cigarette in her mouth and drew on it with her eyes half closed.

"God, the possibilities!" the boy said. "I mean, they don't *end!* I mean, they're *infinite!* There's nobody doing anything *like* it! I mean, you don't reject the gift of serendipity!"

Laurel gazed at J. Dan and said, "He wants to go. He wants me to go with you, and he wants to come along too. He's a film maker. He makes all these far-out films that you wouldn't know anything about, J. Dan, because you two inhabit like totally different worlds. But anyway, that's what he does. He directs, takes the pictures, edits, conceives . . . the whole bit."

"God, I'd like to take pictures from the back," the boy said, frowning at J. Dan and shaking his head sideways.

"You mean from the bed?" J. Dan asked.

"Absolutely. Right over the top of the cab."

"It's the craziest thing in the world, just about," Laurel said in a tired voice. "But then so's he, I guess." She paused again and frowned harder.

Then, as if uttering a difficult axiom, she said, "But if Jeffrey goes along, it's all right with me. On condition, that is: I'm not going to stay at the house. Or even *go* there."

"How about it?" the boy asked, looking at J. Dan instead of Laurel.

19

"Hell, I guess it's all right with me, too," J. Dan stated, nodding his head.

"You don't know what you're letting yourself in for," she said.

"I reckon I can handle just about anything that comes up," J. Dan said. "If the only way to get you to come with me, short of tying you up and throwing you over my damn shoulder, is to bring him along, why that is what we will just about by God have to do. Sometimes a man has to do what he didn't count on to get the right thing done. So it's all right with me."

"Are you sure?" Laurel asked.

"Sure I'm sure," J. Dan said. "If it's money that bothers you, why forget it."

Laurel smiled a little. "No, that's not what I was thinking of."

But J. Dan didn't seem to hear. He rubbed the heel of his hand in his eye and yawned. Then he said, "Never mind, I'll take care of that. I've got me a roll. All I am here to see to is that this girl gets back and says good-by to her mother. That's the least I could do. It's about time I do something decent, it seems to me."

Laurel took a wisp of her hair, put it under her nose like a mustache, and said, "I noticed you've been saving up."

Then, when he didn't respond, she said, "J. Dan's been my proud and highly moral dam's boy friend for . . . how long, J. Dan?"

"About six years, I guess."

"About six years," Laurel repeated. "And I lived there with you pair of horny, self-righteous lovebirds for two of them, didn't I, J. Dan?"

"Now listen here, there is no damn sense in talking like that," J. Dan said. "You know damn well what the situation was: your daddy, he simply disappeared, and there wasn't no way your mother and I could have gotten married. We were married in the sight of God, is the way we figure it. And my first wife died. So that is just the way it was, and there is no damn sense you giving this boy the impression it was something dirty, because it wasn't, and you damn well know it."

"Why do you call him a boy?" Laurel said, leaning forward. "He's twenty-seven years old, and he's done more in those twenty-seven years than most people dream of."

"Maybe," J. Dan said slowly. "Only maybe some people wouldn't *want* to do all them things."

"You better watch him, Jeffrey," she said. "He's not as dumb as he sounds."

"If you was mine, you wouldn't talk like that," J. Dan said.

"Who does he remind you of, Jeffrey?" Laurel asked.

Jeffrey looked at J. Dan and said, "I don't know. Who?"

"There was a bit player in the old westerns. You used to see him all the time. He'd be one of those stereotyped heavies, you know? The same build, the same rugged face. Maybe he was just an extra, or maybe a stunt man."

"Well, is it a deal?" J. Dan said, raising his chin and squinting at her.

"I want to get all these like sky shots," the boy said. "You know, with the pickup structuring the space, centering it . . . tying it down and giving it a place."

"You mean you make *money* taking these here pictures?" J. Dan said.

"It's been known to happen. I mean, I don't fight it."

"You take that one?" J. Dan asked, motioning his thumb toward the lady and the chimpanzee.

The boy glanced at it, and shook his head. "No, that was some other stud. But I mean, it's really something else, isn't it?"

J. Dan nodded, and Laurel said, "He hasn't been able to take his eyes off it, have you, J. Dan?"

"It is not exactly the kind of picture a man sees ever day," J. Dan said.

"Well," Laurel said, "if we're going to go, we'd better get started, I guess."

"That's right," J. Dan said.

"Wow!" the boy said. "Christ!"

"Do you have plenty of film?" Laurel asked.

"I think so," the boy said. "I've got eight hundred feet; that ought to give me like *shooting* room. At least on the way out."

"It won't take you long to get ready will it?" J. Dan asked.

"No," Laurel said. "We don't have to pack very much. If you don't have much, you can't leave much behind."

"That's good," J. Dan said.

Then Laurel frowned and said, "Oh, I almost forgot. This is Jeffrey Martin. Jeffrey, this is J. Dan Swope."

J. Dan held out his hand and said, "Pleased to meet you," and Jeffrey Martin stared at the hand for an instant, before looking away and taking it, and saying, "Sure. I mean, me too."

5 J. Dan sits in the dark room before the enlarged photograph of the naked lady in pince-nez glasses giving suck to the chimpanzee dressed in a tuxedo. Still no lights have been turned on, and he sits there in the darkness, holding his Stetson in his lap and chewing slowly on a jawful of Redman, trying to remain awake.

Something stirs deep in his gut, and he feels loose, heavy cords twisting and tightening down there, and he knows it won't be long before he has to go to the toilet. He wonders vaguely where the toilet is. His tired eyes burn.

Somewhere in a back bedroom, there is the sound of one of them moving around, packing. Either it is Laurel or Jeffrey Martin; J. Dan cannot tell which.

Then, a few minutes later, someone has put a record on a record player, and a deep visceral bass booms throughout the house, making the floor beneath his feet throb and shaking the naked lady on the wall. Still the aquarium is devoid of fish; still it blows bubbles up through the lettuce grass in the tank.

The house smells of cats, unwashed clothes, stale cigarette smoke, and rancid bacon fat. Everything around him is filthy, and J. Dan holds his Stetson firmly on his lap, keeping his spine straight so he doesn't fall off the damn chair.

The melody has no shape, but the bass continues to pulsate throughout the house, drumming away at J. Dan's alertness. And his loosening bowels.

He has to stay awake until he gets them both in the truck; then, when he gets them on the right road, pointed in the right direction, he can let one of them drive, and he can relax and get himself some shut-eye. But only then. They are as unstable as a bucket of dynamite caps; they are as unstable as propane gas. J. Dan can tell. He knows damn well they cannot be depended on for any damn thing.

Kicks. That's what they're out for, kicks.

But goddammit, he will bring her back. Yes, he will by God bring back the long-legged, buck-toothed, big-titted puppy bitch to say good-by to her mother, if it is the last damn thing he does.

Yes, by God.

The bass pounds and jars the insides of his calves, the outsides of his legs, the heavy jowls, the tumbled tired belly hanging over the soft cowskin saddle-leather belt.

Because it has got to be.

Florence, hang on, because we are coming.

And I have got to take me a shit something fierce.

J. Dan stands up and takes two steps toward the kitchen. His leg and back are stiff. He calls out, "Where is the bathroom?"

Laurel sings back that it is at the rear of the kitchen, the door on the right, and J. Dan staggers once and then goes back and goes through the door into a little room the size of a damn telephone booth and drops his pants and sits down and relaxes his bowels and lets it all tumble loudly out the back end then.

The bass wows in again and there is an electric guitar and

J. Dan tries to think of that fellow he once knew in Casper who played the guitar like a damn fool.

He is relaxed and warm all over, and then he notices there is a little electric heater right there before his foot, his damn pants squeezed up like an accordion about his ankles shoved almost into the red coils, and it is breathing out warmth upon his naked legs.

And he is so damn relaxed that he mumbles out loud, and then falls asleep sitting upright on the damn toilet.

6 "Hackensack," Jeffrey Martin said.

"What?" J. Dan asked.

"New Jersey," Laurel said. "That's where he's from. You asked Jeffrey where he's from, and he told you."

"Wrong," Jeffrey Martin said. "That's only where I was born. I was raised in the Bronx."

"That's in New York City," Laurel said.

"I know where it is," J. Dan said.

"I just thought I'd tell you in case you didn't," Laurel said. She took a strand of her hair and made a mustache with it. Identical solid, black loose-leaf notebooks lay in Jeffrey's and her laps.

J. Dan narrowed his eyes, and then opened them wide again. The western prairie rolled, undulated, evaded the eye's desire to measure and record the distance and location of things. The weather was funny, sure as hell. And the light was funny; even J. Dan, with his tired and burning eyes, could see this. And he could smell the two of them, crowded in the seat beside him.

Two hours before, they had followed him out the front door, Laurel carrying a knapsack by the straps and Jeffrey fiddling with his camera. When J. Dan stopped to spit by the right front fender, Jeffrey almost bumped into him, but he stopped in time, not even looking up from the camera. Laurel went around in back and slung the knapsack into the truck bed alongside a bale of hay, a ring of barbwire, and a roll of dirty canvas tied with rope.

"Look at them," Laurel said, "they're like gigantic gray ski tracks. I mean, the road is. The double highway, the way it stretches over those hills."

"Those aren't no damn hills," J. Dan said. He was groggy.

"You sure you're all right," Laurel said. "I mean like *wide awake?*"

"I am doing just fine."

"Jeffrey or I will drive whenever you want."

"Driving Betty Bump," Jeffrey said, shaking his head and grinning.

"I am all right," J. Dan muttered.

"God, I'll never forget it," Laurel said.

"Forget what?" Jeffrey asked.

"J. Dan falling asleep taking a *shit!* I mean, God, that was the funniest thing I've ever *seen!*"

Jeffrey laughed briefly, and then there was the whir of his movie camera as he pointed it straight ahead at the highway.

"The funniest thing I ever saw in my *life!*" Laurel shrieked. She reached over and patted J. Dan's hand. "I never realized you were so lovable," she said.

"I am happy to oblige," J. Dan said, hardly opening his lips.

"Look at those telephone poles," Laurel said. "They're like crosses on some infinite Gethsemane." She opened her notebook and wrote in it.

"Oh God," she said, closing it. "I'd forgotten the size of it all . . . the like *austerity!*"

Jeffrey lowered the window and added to the sudden contralto whir of the wind the lesser, treble whir of his camera.

"Close the damn window," J. Dan said.

"Sure," Jeffrey said a few seconds later, and rolled it up.

"It *is* sort of cold," Laurel said.

"It isn't the cold," J. Dan explained, "it is just I don't like all that damn air coming down the back of my damn neck."

"Sure," Jeffrey said. "Magpies, hawks. More hawks than I've ever seen before. Do you know what kind they are, J. Dan?"

"Chicken hawks," J. Dan said.

"Red-tailed hawks," Jeffrey said.

"They're all the damn same to me."

"Snow fences like fragile Venetian blinds," Laurel whispered, "or Chinese screens."

The truck swerved to the shoulder on the right, and Laurel said, "How long do you intend to drive, and risk getting us all killed just because you're too stubborn to admit you're sleepy?"

Without looking to the side, Jeffrey places the camera in Laurel's lap, on top of her notebook, and she accepts it without a glance at either him or the camera. Her fingers grope loosely about it to keep it from falling. She knows without looking that he has put the lens cap on.

Jeffrey opens his notebook and punches his ball-point pen. Then he patiently begins to print words in the notebook, sentence after sentence down the page. Laurel watches him for a while, interested once more in the fact that Jeffrey has never really learned handwriting, or tried to learn, but continues to print his notes . . . all of these years after leaving those progressive schools where he first learned to print, and no one ever tried to force him to learn handwriting, or anything else that contradicted his spontaneity.

Now he is frowning in concentration, and when he has almost reached the bottom of the page, Laurel reads what he has written:

THE MUSICAL SCORE INHERENT IN THE FILM . . . HEAR IT AS OTHERS CANNOT. SILENCE IS WHERE REAL ORCHESTRATION HAPPENS.

POUND LIGHT LIKE RUMPLED TIN INTO SHINY FLATNESS OF THE SCREEN.

AM HAUNTED BY THE UNSEEN FILM THAT LIES DISCARDED (DISJECTA MEMBRA) ON CUTTING ROOM FLOOR. WANT TO CARRY SENSE OF THIS UNREALIZED POWER INTO EVERY SCENE.

"You two doing your schoolwork?" J. Dan asks.

Laurel raises her face and looks at J. Dan's image in the mirror without answering.

Jeffrey turns the page, also ignoring J. Dan's question. Laurel can hear him breathing as he prints word after word, trying to articulate the flow of his ideas.

J. Dan opens the batwing window again, and then closes it a little. He can't seem to adjust it right. His face feels swollen, hot, and prickly.

Laurel starts to whisper the words of a song titled, "There's a New Man and Woman Born This Day." Her voice is warm, gentle, fuzzy, as if she is entertaining herself privately.

Jeffrey writes:

FILM MAKER AS ALIEN. HE COMES FROM WITHOUT AND ROBS THE CULTURE OF ITS SACRED TOKENS, BEAUTIES, TRUTHS . . . BUT ONLY ULTIMATELY TO REVEAL THEM AGAIN . . . TO FRAME THEM AS THEY SHOULD BE FRAMED. IT'S ALL EVIDENCE. LIKE, WHEN HE WAS IN JAPAN, FENOLLOSA WROTE: "I HAVE BOUGHT A NUM-BER OF THE VERY GREATEST TREASURES SECRETLY. JAPANESE AS YET DON'T KNOW I HAVE THEM." THIS IS WHAT I'M DOING. NO ONE HAS SEEN IN MY WAY BEFORE.

WHY SHOULD THEY? HAVE TO ANSWER THAT. WILL.

FILM IS TRUE MIRROR IN ROADWAY (STENDHAL). BUT MOVING MIRROR OF MOVING PAGEANT.

7 "I admit that I am sleepy, all right," J. Dan stated, opening his eyes wide and taking a deep breath.

Laurel switched on the radio, and said, "Maybe this will help keep you awake."

27

"It will if you get something worth hearing," J. Dan said.

Laurel tuned in a country-and-western song, with two girls singing a duet with guitars and an electric organ in the background. J. Dan nodded, and then, when he happened to glance in the center rear-vision mirror (which he kept in the pickup along with two side mirrors, because, he said, a man ought to see *every* damn thing that's going on), he got a quick glimpse of Laurel's face, and was surprised to see that she was looking back at him. She suddenly crossed her eyes and stuck out her tongue at him. J. Dan didn't condescend to notice, but eased his tired eyes back to the road, where they belonged.

But there was no doubt: there was something sure as hell wrong with that big puppy bitch. Not a damn bit like her mother in a million years.

"I don't believe I recognize that song," J. Dan said, shaking his head no as if answering a question.

"It's probably called 'Any Way Will Do,'" Laurel said. "At least, that's what they keep saying over and over. And I mean they're *right*, you know?"

J. Dan nodded, and then the song ended, and Jeffrey said, "J. Dan, you're too much. I mean, *really too much*, man!"

"Too bad you can't take it," J. Dan growled, and Laurel laughed, and then Jeffrey laughed, too. J. Dan's vision thickened, and he took a deep breath and tensed his arm and shoulder muscles to stay awake.

Another song came on then, and J. Dan said, "Chet Atkins and his guitar."

"Accompanied by Betty Bump," Jeffrey said.

J. Dan wasn't sure he heard right, but it didn't make that much difference, so he nodded anyway.

Laurel started humming with the song; J. Dan opened his batwing window again, to let the cool air wash over his face, and took deep breaths.

When the next song came on, J. Dan said, "Kitty Wells."

Jeffrey opened his window and shot some more film, at some

unknown object. Laurel turned the radio down a little, and then eased her head back against the seat and stared wide-eyed upward.

"The time has come," J. Dan declared in slow judicious tones, "when I think I am going to have to have me a little damn drink."

Laurel turned her face toward him and said, "Same old J. Dan. Lovable old, sweet old, decent old, having-his-whiskey-at-ten-in-the-morning old J. Dan."

"When you get done talking, reach over there in the glove compartment and get me out one of them bottles of Old Charter."

Laurel rested her forearm on Jeffrey's knee and punched the glove compartment open. Then she took out the pint bottle that was only half full.

"And help yourself," J. Dan said. "You and your boyfriend over there. That is, if you're not too damn *good* to take a drink."

"No thanks," Jeffrey said, looking out the window. "Too early, man."

Laurel unscrewed the top and took a sip before handing the bottle to J. Dan.

J. Dan glanced in the rear-vision mirror and, seeing that no car was about to pass, tilted the bottle into his mouth and swallowed vigorously. Then he wiped his arm across his mouth and sighed, filling the cab with the warm smell of bourbon.

"Damn!" he said, and handed the bottle back to Laurel. She looked at it an instant, and then screwed the top on and put the bottle back in the glove compartment.

"It is pretty damn early for that, I'll admit," J. Dan said. "But sometimes a man needs himself a little help and comfort."

"Sometimes he needs it pretty often," Laurel said.

Jeffrey was leaning over and running the camera at the rear-vision mirror, holding it in front of Laurel's face, with one of his arms around her neck.

"Stop it," Laurel said, "you're about to like *suffocate* me!"

29

J. Dan almost dropped off, and he shook his shoulders vigorously, dimly alarmed at what had happened. He gripped his hands on the steering wheel.

"We need gas anyway, so I am going to get me a cup of coffee," he said. "Didn't I see me a Stuckey's sign back aways?"

When neither of them answered, J. Dan said, "I think maybe I did."

And then, a few minutes later, there was the big Stuckey sign, and half a mile after that, the turnoff.

When he was about ready to turn left on the overpass bridge to go to the filling station, Laurel said, "How's come you're so sleepy, J. Dan?"

"I haven't been getting me any damn sleep," he explained. "I have been staying up with Florence, and then I had to take a sick yearling bull to the vet and he wasn't there, and then I had to go to my bank day before yesterday to get me some money, because they told me she wasn't going to make it this time for sure . . . that's when I called you the first time. As a matter of fact, Saturday night I played me some damn poker at Bill Banks's place and when you get to be *my* age you don't snap back the way you used to. And then I drove all night last night, because I got me a late damn start. What with all the fuss and worry, I don't figure I have gotten me over eight or ten hours of damn sleep in the past three days, and I am just about done in."

They pulled into the station and got out of the pickup. Laurel leaned backward and stretched her arms, letting her CPO jacket fall open, and then she saw something that straightened her up.

"Look over there," she said to Jeffrey. She nodded in the direction of a little fellow standing at the entrance some thirty yards away. He was dressed in a British military greatcoat that hung below his knees. The sleeves were rolled up four or five inches, and the coat was mossy and almost iridescent with filth and age. There was a pale area high on each sleeve where corporal's chevrons had once been sewn. His head was covered with a nimbus of teased kinky hair that circled the little pink face without differentiation as beard, sideburns, mustache, and hair, so that the greatcoat seemed to be topped by an enormous dusty-tan thistle, with a face like a meaty little bud at its center. He had a guitar slung by a piece of clothesline over his left shoulder, and was holding a sign saying DENVER in his hand. He was standing there looking back at them out of wire-rimmed granny glasses.

"What in the hell is it?" J. Dan asked.

"I'm going over to talk to him," Laurel said. Jeffrey followed her several steps behind, and J. Dan said, "Well, if anybody asks, I'm going inside," only neither seemed to hear him.

When she was about six paces away from him, the little man flashed the peace sign, slowing Laurel up slightly. His eyes were level with her mouth, but the top of his hair reached as high as her head.

"Are you going to Denver?" she asked.

The man nodded and pointed at his sign.

"Play something," Laurel said.

The boy smiled and put his Denver sign down on the asphalt. Then he looped the guitar around his neck and, to the accompaniment of a heavy strum-and-slap, sang:

Evil, Baby, spelled backwards . . . is "live";
If you're gonna take, you have just plain got to give;
If you're gonna give, you know you're gonna do wrong;
If you're gonna do wrong, you're gonna someday
    he-hear my song:
Evil, Baby, spelled backwa-a-ards is "live!"

Jeffrey had his camera up and started filming. The boy nodded, his glasses flashing, and started singing another to the same slap-and-strum:

I'm gonna take my mixed-up mind and make it go;
I'm gonna run it up to the pump at Sun-o-co;

I'm gonna have it filled right up with real high test;
And clean the windshields of my eyes where they been
   messed
By all them funky birds flyin' overhead.
I'm gonna get it all together, like I just said;
I'm gonna turn it on and take off, Baby, slow;
I'm gonna take my mixed-up mind and make it go!
I'm gonna run it up to the pump at Sun-o-co.

"God, that's cool," Laurel said, laughing.

Jeffrey lowered his camera and grinned.

"What's your name?" Laurel asked.

"Peter Peters," the boy said, shaking her hand.

"You've got to be kidding," Laurel said.

"No," Peter Peters said. "I'm not kidding." He smiled, showed a missing tooth, then closed his mouth. The wind staggered and shifted suddenly, and for an instant the three of them seemed to be closed off from the air, smelling like the used-clothes bin in a junky old secondhand store.

"Sing another one," Laurel said.

Peter Peters raised his guitar and said, "This is called 'The Rock of Ages Rock' ":

> The Universe is a big guitar,
> And it's stru-hummed by God!
> The Universe is a big guitar,
> And it's stru-hummed by God!
>
> I can hear it in my ears,
> The Music of the Spheres;
> It's almost too much,
> I feel my head is losing touch!
>
> The Universe is a big guitar,
> And it's stru-hummed by God!

I can feel it in my bones,
Those celestial tones;
They unravel my mind,
E-he-hevery time!

The Universe is a big guitar,
And it's stru-hummed by God!

"Come on, let's go," Jeffrey said.

"As a matter of fact, I *am* hungry," Laurel said. Then she said to Peter Peters, "We'll give you a ride when we finish here, if you want, only we're only going across the Colorado border. Okay?"

Peter Peters smiled and once again flashed the peace sign at them, and then leaned over and picked up the Denver sign.

Laurel walked past the filling-station pumps, under the overhang, and into the restaurant. J. Dan was just emerging from the men's room.

"Where's he going to ride?" Jeffrey asked, before J. Dan was close enough to hear.

"Never mind," Laurel said. "We'll make room somehow."

"I could eat me a damn horse," J. Dan said, coming up.

They followed him to the counter, where he ordered three plastic-wrapped ham-salad sandwiches, three ham-and-cheese sandwiches, three large coffees, and a package of ten Hershey bars.

"They went to an eating counter and ate standing up, listening to the jukebox playing the Carpenters' singing "A Ticket to Ride.""

"God, I can't believe he's for *real!*" Laurel says out of her last mouthful of ham salad, when the record had finished.

"Who's for real?" J. Dan asks.

"Nobody, J. Dan. I mean, I'll tell you after a while, because . . . well, never mind. If you're meant to know, you'll know."

"I hope I'm not meant to know is all I can say."

When they finished, J. Dan went to the counter for another cup of coffee to go, and Laurel and Jeffrey went outside. Peter Peters was gone.

"He's gotten a ride," Laurel said. "Well, I'm glad of that, at least. Only I wish we could have talked to him some more. I mean, he was really too *much!*"

Jeffrey was standing by the right front fender of the pickup, taking J. Dan's picture when he came out of the restaurant carrying coffee. J. Dan merely nodded at him, then removed a toothpick from his mouth and said, "Sure must be an exciting damn movie you're getting."

"You have no idea," Jeffrey said, putting the cap back on the lens.

J. Dan threw the toothpick away and then shook his head as he gazed into the distance. A wind agitated graying spikes of hair below his Stetson.

Getting back into the pickup, Jeffrey asked J. Dan what the rifle hanging on the rack in back of the seat was.

"That is a 243 Winchester," J. Dan said.

"No, I mean what's it like *for?*" Jeffrey said.

"It's for just damn near about anything," J. Dan said. "Coyotes, jacks, varmints generally. Best damn coyote gun there is. Only I don't hardly ever shoot one any more. They are not the pest they used to be. A man has got to be realistic."

J. Dan started the engine and they glided away from the pumps, back onto the bridge, and once more out onto the highway.

"Of course, every now and then I take my two dogs out and let them run themselves a coyote. Blows out their damn tubes, let me tell you! I mean, them coyotes can really smoke when they take a mind to. Of course, my dogs will catch maybe two out of three. They're fast and they know how to work together. They really tear hell out of one when they get him!"

"What kind of dogs are they?" Jeffrey asked.

"Greyhounds. Only kind that can catch a damn coyote. Both

34

fawn-colored, and as alike as two peas in a pod. Stranger and Scratch is their names."

"Who's taking care of them while you're on this crazy trip?" Laurel asked.

"Bill Banks," J. Dan said. "One of my old poker buddies. He's seeing to the dogs and cattle both."

"You don't shoot coyotes with that gun any more?" Jeffrey asked.

"Not when I am running my dogs, I don't," J. Dan said. He fingered some chewing tobacco into his mouth as he guided the wheel with his elbows. "That is some damn rifle, though."

"Yes, I imagine it is," Jeffrey said distantly.

"I killed me a big mule deer with it a couple years ago," J. Dan said.

"J. Dan," Jeffrey said, shaking his head and smiling, "you're too much, man."

"If he don't stop saying that," J. Dan said, to no one in particular, "I'm going to have to bust his damn ass for him."

"Now boys," Laurel said, in her old-lady voice, "no fighting. It's certainly a good thing I'm here between you."

"J. Damn," Jeffrey said. "J. Damn, J. Damn!"

"Jeffrey," Laurel said, "why don't you shut the fuck up?"

J. Dan nodded. Jeffrey smiled, distantly, closed his eyes, and leaned his head against the window.

Soon they were doing seventy again, and J. Dan opened his batwing window and took a chew of tobacco.

"Still sleepy?" Laurel asked. "Didn't that little stop help?"

"The coffee helped a little damn bit," J. Dan said. "But the truth is, I am still dog tired."

"You should have picked up some No Doz, or something," Laurel said.

"I don't mess around with drugs of *any* damn kind," J. Dan stated.

Laurel grinned and said into the center rear-vision mirror, "You've really got to be kidding!"

35

When he didn't answer, she said, "Why don't you let one of us drive?"

J. Dan frowned and said, "Maybe I will have to before long."

"The thought doesn't seem to turn you on," Laurel said.

He glanced in the mirror, but she wasn't looking at him this time. She said, "I mean, you really *look* tired, you know?"

"I don't doubt it," he said. "I feel like I'm about to trip over my eyelids every damn step I take. But what the hell, there's plenty of damn time to sleep after you're dead."

"That's always a comforting thought," Laurel said.

They passed a sign that said TEX FLOW—GOOD PIPE—MORE IRRIGATION FOR YOUR MONEY.

"When you see signs like that," J. Dan said, nodding, "it means you are getting near home."

"How near are we?" Jeffrey asked.

"Oh, a couple hundred miles yet," J. Dan said. "Maybe a little over. But we are sure as hell getting near."

"I wish I hadn't come," Laurel said. "Honest to God, I feel like I'm like *hallucinating!* I mean, just what in the fuck are we *doing* here?"

"It has got to be done," J. Dan said. "Some things are just right, and there's nothing you can do about them one way or the other. Maybe if you are ever lucky enough to grow up you will understand. They are just right. Some things you *like* to do; some things you *have* to do."

"Like I say," Jeffrey said, "you're too much, J. Dan."

"Keep still, Jeffrey," Laurel said, patting his thigh. Then she started pulling at a pale raveling from a small tear in the jeans, kneading his leg.

"This country is really fantastic, though," he said, his voice slightly hushed. "Truly, truly," he whispered.

"I still wish I hadn't come," Laurel said. "Nothing is right. I feel it. I mean, it's like everything is on the wrong reel. You know? I mean, my head's so fucked up, and yet I have this terrible sense that I'm *imprisoned and don't know it!*"

"Everything is *on the right reel*," Jeffrey said. "The right metaphysical reel! Let the script happen. That's why we're here."

"Pirandello?" Laurel asked. "Are you still on *that* shit?"

J. Dan dozed off infinitesimally, causing the pickup to nose briefly toward the berm.

"Easy," Laurel said, but she said it dreamily, as if she didn't really care. Then she opened her notebook again, and wrote:

Sandy hills rolling away from the road, tufted by dry little clumps of vegetation in the crotches of the land. Like pubic hairs. Funky, sloppy Mother Nature. Doesn't give a shit. And why do I always think of windmills when I remember home? They're standing all along the ridges, watching us go by. I can't remember my real father. (So the windmills are phallic, Laurel, does that surprise you?) But why do I think of windmills, and why do they stand there in my dreams? It's uncanny that Jeffrey has picked up on them. Like, they're very much part of the film he's doing. So maybe we've got it together, he and I. Now if I could only get my head together. If I could only get back to my poetry and do something I could be really proud of. Guess I'll just have to keep on trying, no matter how much it hurts and frenzies the mind.

She closed her notebook simultaneously with the whir of Jeffrey's camera. Once more J. Dan's head eased forward and he almost dropped off to sleep. The truck swerved to the side.

"Great idea," Jeffrey said. "That's it, stop."

"He's not stopping for your sake," Laurel said, scratching the back of her head.

"I reckon I will have to give in and turn her over to one of you," J. Dan stated in a deliberate voice. "I can't keep my damn eyes open another damn second."

When the pickup stopped on the berm, Jeffrey opened the door, got out, and climbed quickly to the fence row at the top of a ten-foot bank. He started to take more pictures of the windmill. Then he turned the camera back in a slow arc toward the truck, and Laurel slowly raised her hand outside the door. It was the slow-motion gesture of a swimmer.

"Where is he off to?" J. Dan asked.

"He's shooting some footage," Laurel said. "He's like *really excited*, you know?"

"Can he drive?" J. Dan asked, looking back and trying to see him.

"Sure," Laurel said, now looking straight ahead.

"Well, make damn sure he keeps right on Route 70. You hear? I'll get me a half hour of shut-eye and then I should be in better shape."

"Sure," Laurel said. "Come on, move over. I'll get out and come around and sit in the middle."

J. Dan eased himself over, and when Laurel closed the door, he leaned his heavy head against it and the back of the seat, pulled his Stetson down over his eyes and immediately fell profoundly asleep.

"Do you ever feel like *trapped?*" Laurel asked. "And don't know why?"

8 Laurel is utterly naked, kneeling in a field of dry, pale grass. Jeffrey is standing fifteen feet to the side of her, his camera in one hand, the other hand clasped to the back of his neck as he thinks. A wind blows monotonously and insistently over the grass. Laurel's sandals, blue jeans, panties, T-shirt, and CPO jacket are scattered in the grass a slight distance away.

"It's cold," Laurel says. "For God's sake, hurry up."

"Look, if you don't want to do it, forget it," Jeffrey says.

"I want to do it," Laurel explains, "but I want you to hurry up, because I am simply, unquestionably, totally freezing my ass."

Jeffrey frowns at her an instant, and then nods. "Okay," he says, "curl around again, like a coyote bitch making a nest out of the grass."

"How do I know what a coyote bitch is like?" Laurel shrieks, scratching at her scalp. Jeffrey laughs and shoots four seconds of her indignant face.

In the distance, there is a grain elevator standing vague and white, like a castle on the horizon, or like a lighthouse on the prairie sea. Somewhat closer, but at least a mile away, there is the barely visible roof of a ranch house, surrounded by desert oaks, dark wind-blasted cedars, and cottonwoods.

The wind whirs a little louder, and Jeffrey says, "Just circle, you know? You've seen dogs do it. The same thing. I mean, just circle around and around. I want to get it low, so all the camera sees is just your head, shoulders, and breasts, but it'll be apparent that you're *circling*. An atavistic nest, you know? I mean, it's like all that happens down below is implicit in the movements of your head, shoulders, and breasts."

Laurel nods, and begins to circle slowly in a squatting dance, and Jeffrey squats, too, taking film.

Over a hundred yards away, the pickup is parked on a thin dirt road, J. Dan sound asleep inside, his Stetson not even visible because he has sunk so low in the seat. One leg is bent, the boot jammed against the opposite door, the other extends over upon the floorboards on the driver's side.

At least, this is the way they had left him twenty minutes before.

Route 70, with its great gray ski tracks upon the land, is not even in sight.

"God, your body is lovely!" Jeffrey says. His eyes are creased almost shut, and he licks his lips.

Laurel sits down cross-legged in the grass and says, "Do it, don't say it."

Jeffrey comes closer and lays the camera on top of her CPO jacket. He is on his hands and knees, and he stretches his head forward and she meets his face with hers, and they touch tongues.

"I'm cold," she says, drawing back with her legs together.

Jeffrey takes his camera off the CPO jacket and hands the jacket to her, and she puts it on, snuggling and shivering.

"It's cold," she says.

Jeffrey moves his hand up the inside of her thigh and shakes the flesh until she loosens. Then he moves his hand under and in.

"Warm," he whispers.

"That's better," she says rapidly, closing her eyes and falling back into the grass, clutching the CPO jacket tightly about her.

"God, what a ball you are!" Jeffrey says, and she laughs with her eyes still shut, as he caresses her again and again, until she is all syrupy and hot and vague, and then he is inside her, and everything starts moving, and the very heavens shake.

A hundred yards away, J. Dan is snoring and chewing on the tasteless damn wad of oblivion.

9 Silently, in the eventual public dream, J. Dan continually approaches the pickup, his tired puffy eyes squinted, his Stetson tilted slightly against the wind.

His face is dark until the image grows into close-up, showing the broken and dented nose, the heavy cheekbones, the deep-set eyes gazing back suspiciously at the lens. The position of the jagged mouth suggests an invisible toothpick, and then it, the toothpick, is suddenly threaded with light.

The wind blows a strand of his graying hair out from behind his ear, tickling the distant sky.

Then there is a single windmill standing like an inverted exclamation mark against the horizon. For eight seconds the windmill turns inside the turning film, the film, at a faster rate, inverting the paddles of the windmill so that they become slow-motioned and sedate; then the windmill itself begins to turn slightly toward the side, withershins, into the light and wind.

A muffled drum has begun to beat, and now J. Dan's face is seen even closer, like the ruins of an ancient temple or city, eventually lap-dissolving into the windmill and the hairy grass of the high bank.

The drum is louder, although still somewhat distant, and a flute or tenor recorder is heard playing a vague melody, stopping periodically for the interval of three drumbeats.

The face returns. J. Dan is speaking into the camera, looking both dismayed and angry under the craggy ruins of his face; but of course his voice is inaudible.

Now there is his profile as he drives. He does not see the camera. He blinks slowly and his head nods forward as if he is sleepily in agreement with some unspoken assertion.

Ruminatively, he is chewing tobacco.

The dream of this scene evaporates like any more common unremembered dream: it exists partially and inchoately somewhere in the camera, in Jeffrey's intention, and in the unfolding actions revealed by the light of each imploding instant.

10 Now the truck was backing almost imperceptibly along the dirt road, and Jeffrey was at the wheel, but leaning out the window and taking film of Laurel Burch as she followed the truck, dragging his CPO jacket in the dust.

The truck lurched slowly and heavily as it went into a low gulley, and J. Dan snorted and woke up. For an instant he sat up in the seat, his hair frayed out and his Stetson hanging crookedly between the back of his head and the seat. Jeffrey had stopped the truck, but he was still taking pictures of Laurel as she approached.

When she was almost even with the front bumper, J. Dan

said, "Where in the hell are we? Where in the hell have we got to?"

"Okay," Jeffrey said to Laurel, stopping the camera. "Come on and get in."

"Where in the hell are we?" J. Dan asked again, squinting his eyes and looking at the dirt road ahead.

"We are in Kansas," Jeffrey said. "Someplace with Betty Bump."

"Don't be such a smart ass," J. Dan said. "Goddammit, I asked you where we were, and I mean to find out. Where are we?"

Jeffrey got out of the pickup and walked around in front to Laurel. J. Dan moved over behind the steering wheel and fixed his Stetson straight on his head.

Then he looked all around, and finally even opened the door and looked behind, as if he couldn't believe the reflection in the rear-vision mirror.

When Laurel and Jeffrey got in the truck, Laurel was in the middle, and Jeffrey was sitting on the outside, doing something to his camera.

"All right, goddammit," J. Dan declared, "I want one of you two shitheads to tell me where we have got to, and I want you to tell me fast."

"The road's back there somewhere," Laurel said, pointing two fingers backward over her shoulder. "I mean, Jeffrey and I decided to shoot some footage."

"God, this open land is something *else!*" Jeffrey said, shaking his head. "I mean, *too much!*"

"I'll show you too much," J. Dan growled, jerking the pickup forward about forty feet. Abruptly he turned the nose up against one bank, and then backed it up, and swiftly turned it around. "How far back there?" he asked.

This time it was Jeffrey who answered. "I don't know," he said. "About ten miles. Maybe fifteen. Listen, man, I mean, we weren't all that long!"

"Shit," J. Dan said, as he accelerated the truck. "Goddammit. Shit. Shitheads. That's what the damn both of you are."

"It's just nice to feel *loved!*" Laurel said in her old-lady voice.

"I'll show you what love is, you damn little slut."

For an instant she was silent. Then, deciding to answer straight, she said, "I mean I already *know* what love is, J. Dan. And even if I didn't, you would be the last fucking person in the world capable of instructing me."

"I will instruct you, all right. I'll hit you over the goddam head and kick your plump public ass if you ever try anything like that again. And that goes for your hairy, picture-taking, turd-faced *friend* over there, too! Understand?"

Neither answered, and the pickup started bucking over a rough place in the road, and J. Dan said, "Shit, a goddam *Jeep* couldn't hardly make it over *this* road! Why in the hell did you come all the way out here, anyway?"

In a quiet, patient voice, Jeffrey said, "The sky, man."

J. Dan shook his head and squinted into the sunlight. Then, guiding with his elbows, he took out his pouch of Redman, wiggled his finger and thumb in the damp coolness until he had a good mouthful, and pulled it out and jammed it angrily into his mouth.

"I do not suppose it would ever occur to you in a thousand damn years to remember that your mother is dying, would it?" J. Dan asked a moment later. His right cheek bulged with tobacco, and his lips scarcely moved when he talked, as if they were swollen and numb.

"I don't remember anything," Laurel said. "And I don't like *want* to remember anything. I've got enough fucking my head up without remembering things and without listening to you, J. Dan. And I mean you *know* it. I told you at the start. This isn't *my* idea."

"Shit," J. Dan said, and spit out the window. "You don't *have* any ideas!"

"You certainly have improved your vocabulary," Laurel said.

"You're almost beginning to sound human."

"Shit."

"Isn't he, Jeffrey?"

"Leave me out of it," Jeffrey said, turning his head away and looking out the window.

"You'd drive a man to it," J. Dan said, shaking his head back and forth, "if anybody would. You're quite a hard little bitch for, what, nineteen? Twenty?"

"I'm old enough," Laurel said. "And I have been old enough for a long time. My proud, clean, loyal, true, dignified, and hypocritical mother saw to that."

"How old are you, anyway?" J. Dan asked seriously a few seconds later.

"Twenty-one," Laurel said.

"The age of consent," Jeffrey said.

"And I do," Laurel said. "I mean, I consent."

"That's true," Jeffrey said, nodding. "She *does* consent. Just about any place and just about any time."

"That isn't nice," Laurel said. "I can't help it if I'm warm-blooded and like devoid of hypocrisy."

"No one asked you to change," Jeffrey said.

"Shit," J. Dan said. "For two damn cents I could bust both of you over the damn head if I hadn't promised your mother I'd bring you to her."

"Shit," Laurel said in a remote voice. "To quote a famous source."

"Maybe if I could have me some dinner, it would wake me up a little damn bit," J. Dan stated.

"Is there a town near?" Laurel asked.

"Nothing but the infinite sky," Jeffrey said, closing his eyes and putting his head back against the seat.

"And the land beneath," Laurel said. "And windmills like great, dried-up sunflowers, nodding over the ranch houses. Or . . . I mean, they're like enormous pinwheels fluttering in the air, abandoned after some impossibly forlorn carnival." She opened her notebook and started writing it down, concentrating with her tongue stuck between her lips and her long hair half screening her eyes.

"God," Jeffrey said, "I'd like to get something of that verbal quality on the film. I mean, it's coming so clear in my mind it half scares me."

"Isn't anybody *else* hungry?" J. Dan asked.

"I can take it or leave it," Jeffrey said. "All I want to do is feel it. And look. It's all coming clear."

"*What's* all coming clear?" J. Dan said, after a pause.

"The film he's making," Laurel explained. "You haven't heard, have you, J. Dan? You're going to be in Jeffrey's film. Along with Betty Bump."

"What?"

"That's right, isn't it, Jeffrey?"

"I don't want no part of your crazy film," J. Dan said. "I don't want no part of *no* damn movie!"

"It's too late," Laurel said, taking a strand of her hair and pulling it over her eyes like a blindfold. "Jeffrey's already been getting you on it. You might as well co-operate the rest of the way."

"What are you talking about?" J. Dan asked.

"For example, he got you when we stopped the first time, and then he shot about ten or twenty feet of you while you were asleep. He's already gotten you on film."

"What kind of crazy damn movie *is* this?" J. Dan cried.

"If it could be explained," Jeffrey said, "it wouldn't be worth doing. I mean, it doesn't necessarily translate into words, you know? At least, the *whole* thing doesn't, although I do want this verbal dimension. All I can say is, it's living film. I mean, we spin it out of ourselves as we're going along. The reality script. The film is the journey, and the journey is the film. You see what I mean?"

"No," J. Dan said. "I sure as hell do not."

"Well, it isn't all that easy to explain. But then, why should it have to be explained at all?"

"Because I want to know what kind of damn *movie* it is!"
J. Dan stated. "Especially if I am going to be in it myself. What
I mean is, I don't want you shooting no damn pictures of me unless I know it, do you understand? You ought to give a man a
chance to prepare."

"But that's exactly what we don't want," Jeffrey said, closing
his eyes and shaking his head back and forth. "No. Some of the
shots can be planned. Okay. I mean, I do it with Laurel all the
time. But the thing is, you've got to play against these. And the
best thing to play against them is the natural thing. Man, I'm
telling you: that shot I got of you sleeping will add up to really
something, you know? You were lying there, crowded up against
the door like your back was broken!"

"I was just plain damn tired," J. Dan said. "Have you ever
been plain damn tired, sonny boy?"

Jeffrey frowned and looked out the side window.

With both hands, Laurel started to scratch her scalp with
long, voluptuous strokes, inhaling with a hissing sound, moving
against J. Dan's arm as he drove.

She was warm and she felt good against him. He sighed and
stretched his eyes wide open in a sudden mad stare, and then
relaxed them.

"I mean, reality is process," Jeffrey said, his voice sounding
farther away, as if he were talking to himself. "So the film is
process, too. It's always just happening, like reality itself, and
then it has to evaporate, like into the past. Doesn't even leave a
trace, man, as it like *boils away*. Volatile."

"I hope you can really exploit some of those ideas," Laurel
said.

"Seems to me I asked you a damn question," J. Dan said.
"Seems to me I asked you if you have ever in your whole damn
life worked hard enough and long enough to get *tired?*"

"That's no question, J. Dan," Laurel said. "And you know it."

"What is it, then?" J. Dan asked.

"It's an accusation."

J. Dan nodded. "Maybe you're right," he said. "But he still hasn't answered."

"It's the nearest thing we've got, you know?" Jeffrey said, shaking his head. "I mean, the director is like God!"

"Must be hard work," J. Dan stated, "being God."

Laurel started singing "There's a New Man and Woman Born This Day." Jeffrey nodded and sighed, easing his head back on the seat.

"You know," J. Dan said after a few seconds, "I am about halfway ready to get me something to eat. In fact, I am downright hungry. I could eat a damn horse, hooves and all."

"I'm getting hungry, too," Laurel said. "Let's stop."

"Not until there's some *place* to stop," J. Dan said. "Damn hard to tell how far you two crackpots drove out from the highway. But there is a town up ahead. I can see the trees and the water tower."

"The trees and the water tower," Jeffrey said absently. "Fantastic title." He put the camera in Laurel's lap and started printing words in his notebook.

"Oh shut the goddam hell up," J. Dan said.

After that they drove toward the town in silence.

11 In the town of Maxton, Laurel sits in a booth inside a small, white frame truck stop and stares at a glass of water. It is hot and cold outside, and hot and cold inside. The weather is strange, full of floating odors and scraping sounds, and suddenly the faces of people look strange to her, like big warped flashlights in a murky season. The lights are seeking her out, trying to shine on her and expose her nakedness. She's sorry she didn't bring her notebook in with her so she could get some of this down. Betty Bump is out by one of the gas pumps, having her tank filled.

Jeffrey is explaining the film. He is pontificating; and feeling his sperm inside her body (or feeling that she feels), she thunders at him silently, wanting him to leave her the fuck alone, wanting to be by herself, alone, alone, alone.

J. Dan has left the table; gone to take himself a damn leak, as he announced, getting up from the table with his big muscular brown hands flat against it, pressing, and then jamming into the table with his leg so that it shook, absorbing the enormous jolt; and then J. Dan walked away, leaving the water swishing back and forth in the glasses, so that Laurel picked hers up and stared at it as it still assimilated the agitation of J. Dan's leaving, while Jeffrey went on and on about the film.

She now realized she was skeptical. Inside, that is. As skeptical inside as she was like *optimistic* and *believing* on the outside. Playing a game with Jeffrey, and maybe with J. Dan, too, only with him it was hard to tell; for example, it was impossible to tell exactly how much or what J. Dan understood. Not that he really made much difference.

That is, she had learned you had to bullshit men, or what was there for a woman? She had learned that later, and going through it in her mind now made her think about her mother. The dying, well-groomed mother. Had *she* bullshit J. Dan? Was that her hold on him, so that he bought her expensive clothes and pampered her and stuck by her when she was dying, and even drove all night to Wichita to get her only daughter, that artsy-craftsy slut (as she'd once called her; was that the last time they'd seen each other?), and bring her, hands tied behind her back, big bobbly boobs thrust forward in a twenty-five-cent Salvation Army T-shirt, frayed from washing and with two holes under the left armpit . . . was that her hold on J. Dan? Of course! Fantastic!

Only where was a woman's honesty to herself as a *person?* Why did she have to act like a pet dog or something?

In the town of Maxton, with filling stations, churches, general stores, three supermarkets, a shoe store, two dry-goods stores, an American Legion hall, an old high school about to be torn down, a new high school on the north edge of town, a Prairie

State Insurance office, two feed stores, two banks, the county courthouse, et cetera.

And a water tower standing one hundred and thirty feet above the ground, a head taller than the cottonwoods all around it digging deep for water and now turning a leathery brown in the leaf. Around the tower in black block capital letters is the name of the town: M A X T O N. The letters almost circle the tower, so that there is no place where you can stand and read the entire name.

"We're getting to him," Jeffrey said, holding his water glass in both hands and staring into it.

"What are you talking about?" Laurel asks, lighting a cigarette.

"Your friend, J. Dan. You know, I think the more we can get to him, the more we are really going to have to work with. You know what I mean?"

"I don't think I do," Laurel says.

"I mean, this whole journey: it's like, well, it's like it exists for the film. I mean, it's actually *becoming* the film. Becoming the action itself. You know, we all lie. That's what reality is, the agreed-upon lie. But you put somebody under pressure, and he becomes like more honest, or at least more intense, more interesting. Every good novelist knows this; and every good film maker. You tug here, and pull there, and the fabric of his unreality, the costume he's wearing, begins to unravel. God, you have no idea! I mean, I can feel it all turning into something stupendous and unreal. Only *more* than real. Surreal. This thing ... this thing is what the real is meant to serve. God! I mean, it's really happening!"

"You make it sound like a fucking game," Laurel says, cupping her glass in both hands and staring at it. Her voice is so low, Jeffrey can scarcely hear what she says next: "I mean, it isn't any game to him; and I can tell you it isn't to me, either."

Jeffrey leans over closer to her and says, "Look, I know that.

It's part of the whole thing; I mean, his *pietas*. You know? I mean, I can see an *Indian* doing this. In every primitive culture there's this passion, this taboo thing, about caring for the dead properly. Like, dying is an act of communication, so far as the living are concerned . . . the survivors."

"I can't see how this relates to the present situation at all," Laurel says.

"It does; it does. And I've got an idea that will really blow your mind. If I decide to use it, that is. Which I don't know yet whether I will or not."

J. Dan comes back to the table once again. He stretches, grunts, and rubs his back, whispering "Damn!" in the direction of no one. Then he jars everything as he bumps his way back into the booth. Laurel watches the water in the glasses as it shakes back and forth from his entrance.

"Just about two quarts and eight pounds lighter," J. Dan says. "I was damn near ready to *drown* in it."

No answer. J. Dan drums his fingers and looks all around the little restaurant, the identical shape and size of a boxcar. Laurel feels the room lurch, and notices that they've moved. No one else notices, but somewhere down the existential line, a blind switchman waves the train on.

"What's taking them so damn long," J. Dan recites. Not a question, a statement of vague impatience. In the last booth back, on the other side, two men in dirty and faded dungarees are sitting drinking Coor's from flip-top cans, their heads close together as they talk conspiratorially. They took a long silent look at Laurel when she walked in with her CPO opened. The interior is dark, only the lighted beer advertisements reflected back from the mirror behind the bar, and long vertebrae of fluorescent lights down the center of the ceiling.

"I am going to get me some more chew," J. Dan says, getting up from the table again in an arpeggio of tremors, the swishing water in Laurel's glass hypnotizing her once again.

"In one sense, we can play him like an orchestra," Jeffrey says.

50

"Christ, I've never seen anyone like him. I mean, he's *unreal!*"

"No, J. Dan's real," she says. "Maybe a little defective, but he's real."

"I mean, it's just right, what we did. Letting him know he's in the film, without knowing how. Or when. Now he's not sure where he's going. He's never quite sure. We've jarred the old cat. And this *is* the film. It's growing right under our hands, and J. Dan's the star. I mean, we've got him like Proteus, you know? And now he'll have to stand still for us and tell us the truth. Christ, what an opportunity! It's like he comes from God, you know?"

Laurel squints at him. "What are you talking about now?"

"All this shit comes from someplace, pussycat."

"What?"

"From God, that's where. I look up into the sky, and I can hear his heartbeat."

"Whose?"

"God's. Who'd you think I meant? J. Dan?"

"Crazy," Laurel says ambiguously, and pulls her hair under her nose. "I mean, I've heard all *this* before, too. God, it's no wonder my head's so fucked up!"

J. Dan comes back, sits down and says, "We have about had time to go out and kill us a damn steer *ourselves* by the time they get us our food."

"Here it comes now," Laurel says.

A lopsided old woman wearing matching tan slacks and sweater brings their order on a tray. Cheeseburgers for everyone, coffee for Laurel and J. Dan and lemonade for Jeffrey. An order of hash browns for Laurel, a bowl of vegetable soup for Jeffrey, and a bowl of chili and a thick piece of banana cream pie for J. Dan.

They start to eat, and are silent for a few seconds, until Jeffrey says, "It's not a film at all. It's a novel. A visual novel, and it's being written right now, right at this minute. It's being *evented*, you know? Instead of *invented*."

"More like an improvised play," Laurel says. "Or maybe like a *happening?*"

"No," Jeffrey says, blowing on a spoonful of vegetable soup. "No, that completely misses the point."

J. Dan shakes pepper into his chili, turning it mostly gray, and asks, "What are you two up to now?"

"It's not just now," Jeffrey says. "It's been happening for a long, long time."

J. Dan blows on his chili and then slurps.

12 Everything comes back to *him*. This thing that is eventing, realizing itself, and that he is riding on, keeps coming back to the blocky old fool sitting on the other side of the booth, looking down into the depths of his chili as he feeds his gut.

Laurel doesn't know, doesn't understand. She sits beside him, and once, halfheartedly, takes his hand and fingers it with her strong little paw. Her thighs are spread before her like a feast, and she is now staring down chastely into her cheeseburger, munching on a squirrel-sized bite, while her fine-spun dirty hair floats about in the darkness like bleached ferns in slow water.

While his faithful Betty Bump grazes outside, the old cowboy sits there with his Stetson beside him on the seat. Jeffrey can't see it, but he can do *better* than see it: the film is happening now, in his mind, and the decision he has to make constantly, from one instant to the next, is how much control must he exercise, how much awareness as they hurtle into the gigantic subject. The subject? The subject is the wind, the sky. It is time and the eventfulness of events. The subject moves, it breathes. Often, it looks exactly like J. Dan. Sometimes not.

The old cowboy . . . what is he, fifty? Fifty-five? The old cowboy sits there, heavy in his gravity, his shirt open upon a hairy chest, his almost bald head tamed by the slab of hand he rubs over it every thirty seconds, in an unconscious parody of the ethics of good grooming, to keep it neat. His wrinkled old eyes turned down at the outsides, so that there is an almost comic look of earnest sadness on that tanned, unthinking face. An oft-broken nose, heavy, brutal cheekbones, a jagged slab of mouth, a bull-neck and thick, high, narrow shoulders. One ear is turned forward, as if wanting to listen, while the other is pasted like a half-crushed wafer against the head.

His old, wrinkled eyes do not lift; he is chewing, bovine from long association with cattle. Marvelous.

"J. Dan," Jeffrey says, "you must have had an interesting life."

The statement, the question, is out, and Laurel turns to look at him, suspicion in her face. He knows she is looking, but doesn't know exactly what for.

J. Dan doesn't stop chewing, but looks back at him calmly, his murky eyes almost suspicious, but not quite. Wary, but so tired they can't see much.

"I have had me a few good times," he says finally, raising his eyebrows synchronously with looking down once again at the remaining clots of chili in the bowl. "Good luck and bad together, like a man has got to expect in this life."

There are a few broken veins in his cheek, and the beginnings on his nose. Tiny reticulations of decay, red as blood (which is what they are). Jeffrey and Laurel had gotten out of the pickup first and had come toward the restaurant, and Jeffrey turned around to see if J. Dan was coming, and saw him still in the truck, caught him in the surreptitious act of tilting the pint bottle of Old Charter into his mouth. But that was all; he wasn't drunk, and wasn't all the way a drunkard. A cumbrously sneaky drinker who might soon be an alcoholic, but was now poised at the edge, looking down at the swift, deep water of despair before him.

"You always been a rancher?"

The question tidies up J. Dan's expression, and he wipes his mouth with his napkin. His eyes go distant and reverent, as always happens when old bastards talk about their youth. Reverence before the cleaned-up memory of those myriad confusions and violences of long ago.

"No," he says, shaking his head to make it clear that he means no. "No, because for a number of years I was a rodeo bum. A bronco tramp."

"Where were you in the rodeo?" Jeffrey asks.

J. Dan's eyebrows go up again, and he says, "Why, you name it . . . just about *every* damn where: from Calgary, up in Canada, clear down to Texas, New Mexico and Arizona. I guess I have done them all."

"What did you do?" Jeffrey asks. "I mean, what did you do in the rodeo?"

"Why, I was about everything," J. Dan says, laying his chili spoon carefully in the empty bowl. "I busted broncs—more than I could count—and I rode Brahmas and bulldogged steers, and the last thing I done . . ." Here J. Dan pauses, and his lower jaw drops a little; it appears that the expression is his version of a laugh, but it isn't certain. "Yessir, the last thing I done, and I done it for almost ten years, was to be a clown. You know, a rodeo clown, which isn't the same thing as a circus clown. No sir, not by a *damn* long shot!"

"No kidding," Jeffrey says, leaning forward slowly, but catching Laurel's upper arm with his shoulder as he does so. She flicks a glance at him, and then eases to the side, half frowning and half abstracted from the conversation.

J. Dan nods and says, "No kidding. I was a clown just about everywhere."

"I never would have believed it," Jeffrey says, and J. Dan shoots a quick look at his face, and Jeffrey says, "I mean, you don't seem like the clown type, you know? I mean, you don't kid or anything, and it's hard to visualize you as a clown."

"He was a clown," Laurel says, lifting her chin and sighing. She has a bored look, like that of someone who is about to change the topic of conversation. But she remains silent.

"There's nothing funny about being a rodeo clown," J. Dan

says, shaking his head and looking at the distant wall. The expression on his face is scholarly. "No sir, you paint that damn big grin on your face and you go out there in baggy pants and suspenders, but damn if you don't earn your bacon and beans. Underneath that big grin, there ain't nothing funny at all. What I mean to say, boy, is you get your ass out there in the arena and sometimes you just plain damn sweat! Yes sir, that is exactly what you do, sometimes. *Sweat!*"

"It must be like *dangerous,*" Jeffrey says, taking a drink of water.

"Let's go," Laurel says.

"It's dangerous enough," J. Dan says, folding his big, meaty hands on the table. "Only it's all right if you know what you're doing. Still, I have broke me just about every damn bone in my body at one time or another."

"Tell him about your many head injuries," Laurel says, lifting her chin again and looking out over the restaurant.

"Hell, they don't bother me too much," J. Dan says. "But I have got me some that *do.* Now take that hand." He unfolds his hands and holds his left one up for all to see; Jeffrey grins and almost shakes it, but decides not to.

"That damn thing never *will* straighten out all the way. Look at the fingers; they just plain won't uncurl. Know what happened to stiffen them in that position?"

"I don't imagine he does," Laurel says.

J. Dan blinks heavily at her twice, but then turns back to Jeffrey and says, "A damn bronc stepped on it one time in Missoula, Montana. Curled the damn fingers around, and if I live to be a hundred, they won't ever straighten out!"

"Shouldn't we be going?" Laurel says, curling a strand of hair in her fingers.

"And I have got me about a thousand of these here cricks in my neck and back," J. Dan continues, shaking his head back and forth, "and I've got me this here damn stiff leg that freezes up on me if I sit in one position too long. Sometimes if I have to drive very far, I get out and stretch the damn thing . . . you know, take me a little walk along the berm and shake the kinks out."

Jeffrey shakes his hand and says, "You're out of sight, man. I mean, you really are!"

"J. Dan doesn't want to talk any more," Laurel says, and Jeffrey looks at her in surprise.

"I don't mind," J. Dan says, looking down at his coffee.

"Only we shouldn't waste time," Laurel says.

At this, both men look at her, but neither speaks, and Laurel closes her eyes and scratches the back of her neck.

J. Dan sips at his coffee, and his eyes go distant again. He seems to be poised on the edge of a dream: this time of the past. His past.

His rugged face is placid, muted, reverent.

13 WANT TO BOX SECTIONS OF LIGHT . . . THIS MEANS AM AS CONCERNED WITH THE BACK OF THE BOX, AS PSYCHOVISUAL LIMIT, AS WITH WHATEVER MAY OCCUPY IT AT THE INSTANT. OR "QUADRI-LATERAL CAGE OF SHOT" (EISENSTEIN). ALSO CONSIDER BERGMAN'S IDEA SHOULD NOT MAKE FILMS OUT OF BOOKS.

B. SAYS FILM, LIKE MUSIC, APPEALS DIRECTLY TO IMAGINATION, SHORT CIRCUITING WILL AND INTELLECT. HOWEVER DON'T SEE HOW BOOK CAN'T SERVE AS PREORGANIZATION FOR EVENTUAL FILM.

EACH FILM IS RESULT OF LONG SERIES OF REFINEMENTS, NO ONE CAN SAY WHERE THIS BEGINS (OR WHAT IS RAW MATERIAL AT BE-GINNING OF REFINING PROCESS). THIS VARIES INFINITELY. CER-TAINLY, FILM MAKER IS MAGICIAN, BUT HE IS ALSO, AND MORE IMPORTANTLY, DEMI-URGE AND EXISTENTIAL ENTREPRENEUR.

REFINE, REFINE. CONSIDER EISENSTEIN'S CONCEPT OF "MAX-IMAL LACONISM." BUT E. DOESN'T SAY WHAT LACONISM IS OF. (THIS CRITICAL.)

THINK I WILL DUB IN VOICES OVER, TO MAKE FILM CONTRA-PUNTAL. LITTLE MUSICAL BACKGROUND . . . MAYBE PULSE BEAT OF

DRUM AND FLUTE OR GUITAR PLUCKING AT MIND. SUBDUED. VOICES RECITING, CHANTING. BECAUSE THAT'S WHERE IT IS, THAT'S WHERE IT'S GOING TO BE AT.

CONSIDER: FILM HAS SURPASSED IN SOPHISTICATION THE STILL PHOTOGRAPH, BUT HAS YET TO REALIZE SIMPLE EFFECTIVENESS (MAXIMAL LACONISM REF. TO ABOVE) AND ELEMENTAL, UNEQUIVOCAL POWER OF THE STILL PRINT. THUS, WANT MY MOVIES TO INCORPORATE STILLS IN THEM, AND PLAY AGAINST THIS USUAL DRUNKEN EXCESS OF MOVEMENT. THE FILM STRIVES TO BECOME EVERYTHING, AND THAT'S WHY IT'S DIFFICULT. ITS ARSENAL OF EFFECTS, HOWEVER, IS OVERWHELMING, AND THAT IS WHY NOBODY UNDERSTANDS DIFFICULTY, OR WHAT IS LACKING.

CULTURALLY, YOU CAN'T SEE WHAT YOU'RE REALLY MISSING.

BUT DON'T KNOW. MAYBE ONE STILL PICTURE AT HEART OF EVERY FILM. METAPHORICALLY, ANYWAY.

MOZART COULD "SEE" HIS SYMPHONIES OUT OF TIME, DURATION, LIKE YOU LOOK AT A PAINTING OR VASE. WHICH MEANS, FOR M. IT WAS ALL THERE, NOTATION AND TIME ARRANGEMENT PRESENT IN HIS MIND AT 1 INSTANT.

NOT SURE. 2 OPTIONS: FILM TO RECORD THE FLUX, OR FILM TO STOP MOTION FLUX, GET IT DOWN, NAIL IT, MAKE IT STICK TO THE MIND LIKE A CANVAS.

FREEZE THE HERACLITEAN FLOW.

WHICHEVER, THIS HAS TO BE EVENTED.

NEVER DESPISE GODDESS CHANCE, UNFORESEEN GIFTS, OPPORTUNITIES THAT TAKE ACROSS THE BORDER.

J. DAN PURE GOLD. DOESN'T KNOW.

I MEAN, LIKE WE WERE MEANT TO COME TOGETHER. FILM AS MYSTICAL EXPERIENCE. WHY NOT? YEATS'S THOUGHTS CONCEIVED IN WHOLE BODY. GESTURE AS REVELATION. EVERY CELL OF THE EVENT FIRED SYMBOLICALLY LIKE BRAIN CELL. YES, THE FILM ITSELF HAS A MIND. BUT NO MEMORY.

THIS IS WHERE I'M AT NOW, AT THIS TIME, IN THIS PLACE.

J. DAN IS WAITING. LET US GO TOGETHER.

14 Since J. Dan almost fell asleep drinking his coffee after the meal, they decided Jeffrey should drive Betty Bump for a while.

"No more damn tricks, now," J. Dan said as he picked a toothpick out of a shot glass by the cash register. The lopsided old lady in slacks and sweater took his money, and gave him change.

J. Dan cast an eye above her head and worked the toothpick deep behind the right molar.

"Say," the old lady said, "that weather sure don't look too good, does it?"

The three of them looked outside simultaneously, as if responding to an electric switch.

"No, looks like they might be a little fuss out there," J. Dan said.

"Nothing like that thing a week ago, I hope," the old lady said. "Did you folks hear about our twister? Why, they had to take all the kids out of our new high school and bring them back to the old one until they can fix the heating unit and the air conditioner and I don't know what all."

"Was anybody hurt?" Laurel said.

"No, wasn't nobody hurt, but there was an *awful* lot of damage. I'll tell you, those things just scare me to death, and I've lived in Maxton all my life! I don't know what the world's coming to!"

"Well, we had better be going," J. Dan said, holding his arms up behind Laurel and Jeffrey as if preparing to sweep them out the door.

"Thanks for the meal, J. Dan," Laurel said.

He looked at her, wondering if she was mocking him, but her expression was too vague. She looked like a little girl dreaming, and J. Dan had an impulse to reach over and slap her cheek gently, and then shake her jaw to see if he could make her mouth ease open and jar her big doll eyes until they could see. And maybe even look out at something. Maybe him. Or her mother.

But he didn't do anything but nod and take two steps toward the door, blinking deeply, still picking at the right molar with the toothpick in one hand, and adjusting the wallet in his hip pocket with the other. His Stetson was far back on his head, showing wisps of hair in front, like a tangle of heavy cobwebs over his baldness.

Outside, he ambled up to the boy who had filled the pickup with gas and settled the bill. The boy was tall and slope-shouldered, dressed in dirty green coveralls, and slack-jawed with interest as he stared at the dirty-looking, braless young girl. His eyes were on her as he punched his coin-changer and returned three quarters and a nickel to J. Dan from his five-dollar bill.

Laurel pivoted slowly away from him, toward Jeffrey, a bored expression on her face. Then she whispered in her old-lady voice, "Hippies! Just look at the *hippies!*"

Jeffrey snorted a brief, mirthless laugh. "Yeah, they don't dig us in the town of Maxton, it looks like."

"I mean, they look at you like you're a fucking *animal* or something," Laurel said disgustedly. "God, they don't see anything beautiful in *anything*. Can you conceive of what a like *prison* this place is? I mean, not that there's anything wrong with animals, or anything. I mean, it's their *attitude*, for Christ's sake."

"I know what you mean," Jeffrey said.

"You can feel it in the air, even."

J. Dan had gone into the filling-station office to buy a new pocket comb. When he came out, he walked over to the two of them and started to escort them back to the pickup. He wiped his hand over his mouth and said, "I want it understood, now. You take off across the country like you done the last time, and I will break your damn head. I am not a shitting you one damn bit, and I want it understood."

"He understands," Laurel said.

"Well why in the hell don't *he* answer if *he* understands?"

He glared at the silent boy, who was now slouching ahead with his hands in his pockets, watching his own feet as they moved forward. From behind, J. Dan shoved his shoulder with his hand, and the boy shrugged forward a rapid step before he regained his balance.

"I heard," he said, without turning around.

"My mother and daddy always taught me to answer people when they said something to me," J. Dan grumbled.

"The sky sure does look funny!" Laurel said in her old-lady voice.

"Winter's coming on," J. Dan said, squinting up at the sky and tossing his toothpick against the left front fender of the pickup.

"Winter's coming on," Jeffrey repeated. "Good title. I mean, God, they're like popping all around."

"*What* is popping all around?" J. Dan asked, opening the right door of the pickup.

"Don't bother listening to him," Laurel said.

"I wouldn't, if I couldn't hear him so damn plain," J. Dan said.

They climbed up into the pickup, Jeffrey behind the steering wheel, Laurel in the middle, and J. Dan scrunched back against the seat and door, pinched in as far as he could get, his Stetson over his eyes and resting on the bridge of his nose.

"I might stop and let Laurel take over, if I want to sit in the middle and shoot," Jeffrey said. "So don't get up tight if you hear us stop. Okay?"

"I won't," J. Dan said. "Just don't try to stop any longer than it takes for her to get behind the wheel, and don't forget the right road back to 70. Hard telling how much damn time we have already lost."

"There might be an invisible narrator," Jeffrey said, and J. Dan raised his Stetson and stared at the boy for an instant before giving a deep sigh and pulling it back over his eyes. The image of Laurel's profile, the pretty little puppy bitch, stayed with him, and he realized for the first time that the girl looked like Florence after all. Except for the thing about grooming and cleanliness, and things like that, she was right now damn near what Florence was many years before, when she was married to another man, and J. Dan had not yet laid eyes on her. Or had laid her.

"The voice will be in counterpoint, you know?" Jeffrey said, as he eased the pickup out into the road. "And it's going to be formal. Iambic pentameter, even, so that the throb will get through without any of the disturbance of the line. I'm getting some of these ideas down in my notebook."

"Beautiful," Laurel murmured, and J. Dan fell instantly, suddenly, asleep.

15 Just as clearly, suddenly out of the oblivion, Florence stands up and faces him. She is wearing the genuine pearl necklace that she's always loved. There is a cat draped over her arm, and she is stroking it with her free hand. The cat is staring back at J. Dan with an alert, poised expression.

Florence says, "What will I do with it, J. Dan?"

Now they are knee-deep in warm water. It is her own kitchen, but it is flooded. She is slightly buck-toothed. J. Dan has never quite noticed this before.

She continues to caress the cat, which continues to stare unblinkingly at J. Dan.

She smiles vaguely.

"Oh, whatever you want," he says slowly, each vowel a yawn. He is tired, and his jaws ache. His back and shoulders ache; he is cramped up into a perfumed drawer, and thick light sifts through the opening, making him want to sneeze.

"How can it be?" he asks, turning his head painfully, slowly to the side. "We never had no flood here before. We hardly even had enough water for the stock, let alone have us a damn flood."

"Maybe I should drop it and put it out of its misery," Florence says. The water is greasy, like cold soup, and light quivers like silk on its skin.

"No," J. Dan says, "don't do that. Just hold it. The water will go away."

"They drown cats when the water gets deep; then the water goes down."

"Sometimes they do," J. Dan says, and the cat grins and licks its hind paw. Florence is still holding it, only she's sinking deeper in the water, her skirt floating all about her hips like rippling, spreading mud—flowering, thickening. "When the cat's away, the damn mice will play."

"Sure it will," Florence says.

"Sure *what* will?" he asks.

Then she is lying in bed, although he cannot see her face.

Her head is smaller and she has a flowered hat on. "I was just testing you, J. Dan," she says.

"Are you sick yet?" he cries. "You're not sick from the damn cancer yet, are you?"

"No," she says, "that won't be for another year or two. You don't have to go after Laurel yet. You won't have to go after her until I start to die."

"God, Florence," J. Dan cries, his neck hurting and his hands gripping themselves so hard he seems to be clutching at the alloy of an abstract pain.

He clears his throat and tries to spit.

The floor is fifty feet away.

Florence smiles beneath the hat, and then she is sitting up looking for something, a kerosene lamp in her hand. Her jaws are struggling as if they are glued together, and she is trying to speak.

Then he is lying down underneath a fence, and a drunken steer is stepping vaguely on his ankle, and buffalo grass is blowing through the sky, tickling his face and ears, and it is dark near the rim.

"Where is the cat?" Florence cries dimly, somewhere out of sight, in the darkness.

16

"Go get his hat," Jeffrey says. "This light is fantastic."

Laurel blows cross-eyed at a wisp of hair tickling her nose and scratches under her left breast, making it nod like a small soft head.

"Right now, while he's asleep," Jeffrey says. He shoves her arm gently, tentatively. "Go on. Right now, before he wakes up."

"No," Laurel says.

"Go on, before he wakes up!"

"No," Laurel says, blowing at the wisp of hair again, and then closing her eyes and smoothing it back off her forehead.

The wind, which blows almost without stopping, has slowed down to a strange warm breeze. For an instant, ten minutes ago, Laurel had been afraid, thinking that maybe everything was running backward, including time.

"I feel like throwing up when I just think about it," she had said to Jeffrey. "I mean, the whole thing's sick, and I *don't want to see her!*" Jeffrey didn't answer, but closed one eye, and looked out of the other at the pickup resting in the deeply rutted road, the roof at the same height as his ankles as he stood on the high bank. He changed lenses, licked his lips, looked up and all around at the sky, and said, "God, it's beautiful! Austere. Uncompromising and obsessive. A little mad, you know?"

"He's going to be like *really* mad if he wakes up and finds out we've stopped," Laurel said.

"Listen," Jeffrey said, "didn't you just now say you didn't *want* to have to face her?"

"Some things you've got to face," Laurel said in a faint voice, and Jeffrey shook his head at the illogicality built into her mind.

"You're beautiful," he said.

"As beautiful as the sky?" she asked, looking up.

"As beautiful as the sky," he said.

"The earth?"

"The earth."

What had stopped them was an abandoned ranch house standing in a little oasis of junipers and cedars, its windows knocked out and its roof silvered by long seasons of weather. A broken windmill stood guard over the scene.

"God!" Jeffrey had exclaimed when he saw it. He braked the pickup, making J. Dan's sleeping head, the top half still covered by his Stetson, nod heavily to the side, and causing him to smack his lips slightly, as if his mouth had tasted something sour.

"Why didn't we see this on the way out?" Laurel asked.

"Because I took the wrong fork back there. I mean, I turned west, and we came out on the other one. No sweat, they both go back to 70. I mean, they *have* to. There's nowhere else to go, as long as we're generally headed south."

"I hope so," Laurel said, and then Jeffrey turned off the ignition, and they both glanced at J. Dan, who didn't move.

"Just a few minutes," Jeffrey whispered. "Come on."

Laurel edged away from J. Dan's arm, and her movement caused him to shrug his shoulders and snort.

"He's all right," Jeffrey said in a low voice. "Come on. He won't wake up."

Then they climbed the bank right there, instead of going fifty feet down the road to the old, weed-choked driveway, and stood for an instant at the top of the bank, staring at the abandoned house and the windmill.

"Run toward the house," Jeffrey said, holding his camera ready.

"I don't feel like it," Laurel said.

"Why not?"

"I just don't, that's all."

Jeffrey stared at her an instant, and then nodded briefly and turned away, and shot a few feet at the late-afternoon sky, lowering the camera toward the house and trees.

"That sky's fantastic," he said.

Laurel closes her eyes and spreads her arms, inhaling deeply and thrusting her chest toward the sky.

"Go get his hat," Jeffrey says. "This light is miraculous."

Laurel blows cross-eyed at a wisp of hair tickling her nose and scratches under her left breast.

"Right now, while he's asleep," Jeffrey says. He shoves her arm gently. "Go on. Right now, before he wakes up."

"No," Laurel says.

17 After that, Jeffrey shrugged and turned away from her, going up to the abandoned house. She watched him disappear behind the thick old cedars, and then she looked up at the inert windmill, frozen by rust and time in an irrelevant gesture.

For this instant, she felt funky and alone, whirring in a cat's cradle between invisible lines of a mute, implicit appeal from J. Dan sleeping beneath her knees in the cooling pickup and Jeffrey, now meandering in an empty house.

Her mind fluttered and turned, and she closed her eyes and breathed deeply, whispering, "Help me, please. Help me." Trying out the sounds.

Then she opened her eyes and walked toward the house, half frightened, half fascinated by its loneliness and the indifference of the ugly cedars as they trembled slightly in the softened wind.

The shadows were getting long, and part of her fear had to do with its getting late, as if she had accepted the inevitability of the journey back to face her dying mother, and wanted to get it over with. As if her mother were simply waiting for her to appear, and then would die, getting that over with, too.

When she went inside the dark enclosure of cedars, the house began to change before her eyes and grow increasingly morbid, increasingly decayed. The windows had been boarded up, but at least one of them had been broken open, and the door itself had been removed entirely.

Jeffrey was standing in the opening, his left hand on his hip, the camera poised in his right. He stood there motionless, and seemed to be listening for something.

In the darkness of the film, Laurel (naked) receives a command and begins to circle in the grass. Then this circling lap-dissolves into the windmill turning once again (these two turnings happening in the illusion of the turning film, still warmed from the explosive illuminations of shaped light into the little rooms of their retention).

Slowly, subtly, almost imperceptibly, J. Dan's face grows out of the windmill. It is slowly, bovinely chewing tobacco, the wrinkled eyes creased against a metaphysical wind that he cannot name, but that carries light upon his features and reveals him to a whole population, an audience of people who will someday know *his* name or at least, briefly, his image.

Then J. Dan's face lap-dissolves into the face of Betty Bump, forming the true Americarriage (the national modern marriage between man and his car, man and the machine . . . flesh and steel made one).

Momentarily, Laurel is forgotten.

Volatile, immediate, and topical, the film is the instrument for forgetting.

Jeffrey stands in the opening, his left hand on his hip, the camera poised in his right.

He is in stop-motion, himself suddenly rendered as an actor

66

in an inscrutable tableau within a more comprehensive drama, upon another reality script.

He seems to be listening for something, and his intelligent eyes, set wide apart in the goatish face, are meditative.

18 Years before, he'd owned this damn electric alarm clock that came on softly, beginning a little hum about as loud as an electric shaver in the next room, and then growing louder until it was an electric drill buzzing hard and angry at your ear, trying to get inside your damn head.

This was the way it was now. Only right before that (as if in retrospect) he could feel the accumulation of cramped strain in his neck, and his clothes twisted around him, and his guts all shoved together, as if they weighed two hundred and fifty damn pounds from breastbone to crotch.

Then the increased buzzing, which made him start; and he woke up, thrusting his face up into the darkness of his Stetson, smelling the familiar sweatband and the old fabric, and then whipping this off to face the dull green silence of the cab, the engine ticking idly as the block still cooled.

Silence. That's what the buzzing had been, and it had lasted for a long time, only he'd been too damn tired to wake up. If the engine had kept running and the pickup had kept moving forward, he would have kept on sleeping for another hour or two.

J. Dan sat up and squinted his eyes into the strange cast of late-afternoon light, taking in the long shadows, the high bank on the right side of the road. He looked at the ignition lock and saw that the key was gone. He slowly rubbed his right hand over his eyes, and then his jaws, and then smoothed down the hairs on the top and sides of his head.

He took a deep breath, opened the door and stepped out of his pickup. He reached back and picked up the Stetson and put it on. Then he saw what looked like an old, unused driveway of some sort about fifty feet up the road, so he walked up toward it until he could see a clump of trees a hundred yards off the road to the right, with an old abandoned house in the middle of it. And a windmill, missing a paddle, and rusted like it had been standing there a thousand years.

No one around, but J. Dan figured they had gone into the house, otherwise he would have been able to see them. He looked at his watch and shook his head, still trying to drink in all the enormity of what they had done.

Likely, they were in the house; or maybe on the other side of it, where he couldn't see them.

He walked up to the house, slowly and quietly, and stepped through the entrance onto gummy old boards. Then he heard Jeffrey, somewhere upstairs, say, "No, the sound is secondary. I might impose a completely irrelevant sound track on it. I mean, it'll *seem* irrelevant, at first, but it won't be, you know? Something like the muted sound of a train going with all my space shots. We'll explore the connections as we make them."

J. Dan walked as quietly as he could to the stairway and eased himself up the steps. On the next to the top step, he saw them in an empty room. Laurel was squatting, drawing in the dust of the floor with her index finger. Jeffrey was leaning against the wall, his chin raised and his eyes closed. His arms were hanging at his sides, the camera hanging from one hand.

The top step creaked under J. Dan's weight, and at the sound, they both looked at him, two young, wild animals, alert and curious, no more afraid than wary and interested.

J. Dan shoved his hands in his pockets, focused as well as he could on Jeffrey's eyes, and said, "Oh, you lying son of a bitch, I am going to shove that goddam camera up your ass! Don't you two pups have any sense at all? Don't you know what *time* it is?"

They didn't move. J. Dan lunged forward into the room and grabbed at the camera, but Jeffrey capered to the side, holding the camera over his head (as if teasing a slow, fat boy), and said,

"Don't! Listen, man, we just stopped for a couple of minutes! What are like *five or ten minutes?*"

"I'm going to by God stomp your ass!" J. Dan yelled, and lunged again. But once more the boy danced away, and Laurel cried, "Don't, J. Dan. For God's sake, leave him alone."

But he was turning again, charging after the boy, who now skipped out the door, holding his camera like a football. J. Dan stared at him out of blurred eyes, panting from the exertion.

"I am going to stomp your ass if it is the last thing I do," he growled, shaking his head back and forth, "and take that camera and beat it into your goddam damn head!"

He lunged out the door at Jeffrey, but the boy once more dodged to the side and danced down the stairway to the room below. J. Dan saw a changed expression in the boy's eyes as the two of them faced each other now. Somewhere in back of him, J. Dan could hear Laurel saying, in her old-lady voice, "Now look, you two, I mean, all this violence isn't doing *anything!*"

"*I'll* show you who'll do anything," J. Dan said, panting.

It was then that Jeffrey lifted his camera, aimed it at J. Dan, and started shooting.

With a yell, J. Dan started down the steps, grabbing the railing in an attempt to vault over it onto the boy, but the railing broke off, and he went plummeting into the wall, and then on down the steps on his back and side.

For an instant, everything was suspended in a little dream: Laurel was at the top of the stairs gazing down at him, J. Dan was lying on his side, panting and blinking slowly in an effort to collect his wits, and Jeffrey was standing ten feet away peering around his camera at J. Dan, as if waiting for him to go into action again. Had he gotten it all on film?

"There is nothing in the damn drugstore," J. Dan said, even more slowly than usual, and pausing to spit fluff from his mouth, "that could kill you quicker than I am going to kill you once I get my two hands on you, you fucking bastard."

"Keep away from him, Jeffrey," Laurel said. "He probably doesn't mean it, really, but keep away from him anyway."

Jeffrey started shooting once again, stepping closer to J. Dan, and then stepping back when J. Dan got up on one knee, put his Stetson back on, and started to rise to his feet.

"Are you all right?" Laurel asked. "I mean, are you *hurt?*"

"Nothing like your boyfriend is going to be," he said, "if I can just get my two damn hands on him."

Once again, J. Dan lunged at Jeffrey, but this time missed him more grievously than ever. Jeffrey circled him, and then skipped out the front door, as if to lure J. Dan out where the light was better. When he was outside, he started laughing, and said, "Hey, J. Dan, you're too *much*, man!"

J. Dan charged out the door toward the boy, who stood his ground with the camera to his eye, shooting right up to the instant J. Dan could have grabbed him. And then skipping aside so suddenly that J. Dan's feet went out from under him when he tried to turn, and he sat down on the ground, panting and swallowing from so much exertion. Finally, after getting his breath, he pushed his Stetson back on his head, twisted around without trying to get to his feet, and said in a gasping voice, "All right, you have made a fool out of me."

Jeffrey, who had come closer, didn't answer, but continued running the camera, getting it all on film.

J. Dan turned his head away, and then finally climbed to his feet.

Laurel was somewhere near. J. Dan heard her say, "The gun. I'll get it before he gets back to the truck!"

And sure enough, she was running ahead of him, her hands sticking up in the air like she was being held at gunpoint, the way women hold their hands when they run. Before he could take five steps, she had skittered over the bank and out of sight.

"They're just too fast for me," J. Dan said, to no one in particular. Once more he spit fluff out of his mouth and slowly shook his head back and forth. His throat burned clear down into his chest from panting, and his body was beginning to ache all over.

By the time he limped back to the pickup, Laurel was out of sight—up over the bank again, probably; back up by the abandoned house with Jeffrey.

J. Dan saw that his rifle was gone. But how did they know he didn't have a revolver in the glove compartment? He had kept a .38 there until only a couple of weeks ago, as a matter of fact, and then he'd taken it out to have new wood grips put on the handle.

Of course, the damned fools ought to know he wasn't really going to *shoot* them. He'd promised Florence he would bring her daughter, her only child, back to say good-by, and, by God, that was what he aimed to do.

J. Dan got in the truck and blew the horn. Once again he noticed that one of them had taken the ignition key. Now why in the hell had they bothered to do that? He opened the glove compartment, took out the pint of Old Charter straight bourbon, and unscrewed the cap. He looked all around, and then took a long hard drink.

He took another swig and blew the horn again. It was getting late, and looked more than ever like a bad storm was coming. His shoulder and back were getting stiffer from the fall, and he worked them around in a circle. He blew the horn again, and asked half aloud, "*Now* where in the hell did they go?" He took another drink, and then replaced the pint of bourbon in the glove compartment.

But they still didn't show up, and finally J. Dan got out of the pickup and climbed up the bank. They weren't in sight, but he knew they had to be in the house. He cupped his hands around his mouth and yelled, "All right. Come on back. We have by God got to get started. I ain't going to do nothing."

When the two of them came out from behind the cedars, the boy grinning, J. Dan looked at the road leading toward the sagging afternoon sun and muttered, "I reckon I will have to drive all the rest of the way myself."

But the thought was discouraging to him, because he was a little bit drunk, and damn tired.

19

POUND SAYS IDEOGRAM ESSENTIAL FOR SOME KINDS THINKING. WANT TO EMBODY THE IDEOGRAM IN MY CONCEPTIONS. NOTE STASIS OF IDEOGRAM. WORK AGAINST AND <u>WITH</u> THIS.

THINK I'LL STOP-MOTION J. DAN, FOR INSTANCE IN WALKING BACK TO PICKUP. FOOTNOTE HIS SIGNATURE. "J. DAN'S DAMN IDEOGRAM."

REDUCE AUDIENCE TO 6-YEAR-OLD MENTALITY (WHICH ABIDES IN ADULT). THUS DAMAGE LINE BETWEEN REAL AND UNREAL THAT PIAGET SAYS CHILD CANNOT MAKE. WHY NOT? WHO SAYS THIS UNDESIRABLE?

LIKE MEPHISTOPHELES, FILM MAKER MUST ACTUALIZE PRIVATE DREAM IN PUBLIC. RELIEVE FAUSTIAN MAN OF HIS LIKE MEMORY/GUILT HANGUP?

BUT ALSO, RAISE ACCIDENT TO LEVEL OF ART. DIFFICULT. TO RAISE IT, HAVE TO THROW IT INTO VAT OF MIND. (FILM RESISTS THIS, RESISTS ABSTRACTION NECESSARY FOR MIND, REMEMBERING.)

IF ONE PICTURE WORTH THOUSAND WORDS, 1 MOVING PIC. IS WORTH INFINITE # WORDS, LIMITED ONLY BY TIME/PATIENCE-OF-AUDIENCE. I CAN THINK OF A VERY WEALTHY MAN WITH PRIVATE FILM SHOWING CONCURRENTLY WITH HIS LIFE (COUNTER-LIFE), AND HE PAUSES NOW AND THEN TO GO WATCH IT (SAY IN ROOM AS PRIVATE AND ISOLATED AS PSYCHE). BUT IT'S GOING ON EVEN WHEN HE'S NOT THERE TO WATCH.

NOT JUST DREAM, BUT COUNTERLIFE.

ROTHA SAYS FILM IS ART OF OBSERVATION BASED ON POETRY. THAT IS, REALITY FOCUSED THROUGH POETIC LENS. WHERE DOES J. DAN STAND WITH THIS IDEA? WHAT POETRY CAN FOCUS HIM? WHAT IS RITUAL THAT GOVERNS HIM?

HE BECOMES MORE AND MORE INTERESTING THE MORE I THINK ABOUT HIM. HE DOESN'T KNOW WHAT HE'S DOING, BUT HE'S DOING IT. ROLE LOOKING FOR SELF TO ACT IT.

GENIUS OF WHAT HAS BEEN CALLED FLAHERTY'S "NONPRECON-CEPTION" (WHICH NEEDS FOR ITS FULFILLMENT MIND TENDING CONSTANTLY TOWARD CONCEPTION).

YES, AND BERGMAN HAD SOMETHING: FILM IS DECEIT AND EXPLOITS A HUMAN WEAKNESS. ACCEPT THIS. SEE ABOVE ON REAL/UNREAL, AND PIAGET.

SPEAKING OF WHICH, MUST KEEP CHILD INSIDE ALIVE. FEED AND NURTURE CHILD AT ALL COSTS. NOTHING POSSIBLE WITHOUT INTENSITY AND, YES, ENTHUS. THIS CHILD BRINGS. LIKE, THE ONE DAN GIFT, WITHOUT WHICH NOT.

20

"The windmills are what I want now," Jeffrey says. "Transparent, image over the wheels of the pickup, turning together. I can get this when I develop. I'm concerned with like *cycles*, the rotary, you know?"

The pickup is once more nosing forward, over a rough section of the road. Laurel wonders briefly if the highway has like *evaporated*; they seem to have been off it for half a day; maybe they're circling. Even the magpies flying over the road ahead look different. As if they *know* something.

As if hearing her mind, J. Dan brakes the pickup and says mildly, "Well, I'll be diddly-damned."

"What's the matter?" Laurel asks.

"This damn road is going straight west," J. Dan says. "Going *this* way, we never *will* get back to 70, even if we drive a hundred damn years."

Sure enough, the reddening sun is low in the sky, at ten o'clock. J. Dan has been driving five minutes staring almost straight into it out of equally red eyes, not thinking about direction. Maybe he's too tired and drunk.

"Maybe we should go back the way we came," Laurel says, in her old-lady voice. "Back to that sweet, cuddly, wholesome, cozy little town of *Maxton!*"

"I always did hate to backtrack," J. Dan says, shaking his head, "but I suppose it is the best thing to do. And if I'm going to turn around, I'd better do it here, because there ain't many places on this road where you can do it."

He swings the pickup wide to the right and then turns the wheel left, backs up, making Laurel and Jeffrey nod their heads as if in mute agreement with his tactics, and then they are backtracking.

The pickup rocks slowly over the last rough part of the road, and Jeffrey says, "The lonely-carnival motif you mentioned, you know? Like, man, the carnival is really over. After all those *rides!*"

"*Now* what's he talking about?" J. Dan asks, spitting a rich gob of tobacco juice out the window afterward, as if to delay or obviate an answer.

"He's thinking of ideas for the film," Laurel says.

"Some film," J. Dan mutters.

"That idea of pinwheels, too," Jeffrey says. "I can get close-ups of a pinwheel fluttering in the wind, the cycle motif, you know, held in the hand of a little girl, and then it will merge with the windmill . . . you know, lap-dissolve into it, and her hair into the grass and the countryside."

"Cool," Laurel says, brushing her own hair back out of her eyes and arcing a look at Jeffrey, who does not see. Then she takes a pack of cigarettes from the pocket of her CPO, shakes one out, and lights it.

"Maybe I should have followed this damn road until it came to something. Couldn't be *too* far to one that connects with 70," says J. Dan.

"Only it ought to be in color," Jeffrey says. "That part. As much as I distrust color effects, that part will be in color. The rest will be black and white; then a *few* shots merging into color, like that one, announcing the motif."

"I mean, how will you *get* color?" Laurel asks, exhaling cigarette smoke. "You don't have anything with you but black and white."

"I'll think of something," Jeffrey says. "Maybe color shots of abstract shapes, blending in with the circular, the cyclical patterns. I can do it. I know."

"I am only glad *I* won't have to watch the damn thing," J. Dan says.

For an instant, Jeffrey is silent, and then he laughs and says, "J. Dan, you *are* the damn thing. I mean, like *this is your life, man!*"

"You do, and I will by God catch you, so help me, and bust your damn head clear down to your nuts."

"That sky," Jeffrey says, and starts shooting. Laurel leans forward, and looks up through the windshield.

"I don't like it," she says. "It doesn't feel right. Nothing does. And you notice something? The *wind* has stopped. Back there at that abandoned farmhouse. I noticed it right before I got back in the truck: the wind had stopped. I mean, that just isn't like *natural* out here in *this* place!"

Now J. Dan himself leans forward over the steering wheel and looks up at the sky. The dirt of the road is burnished from the fierce slant of the sun under a shelf of black cloud—a whole, solid, inert continent of darkness that has been growing there above them, beyond their notice. The prairie all around is suddenly like an enormous, drafty, overlighted cave. The scars made by the tracks in the road glint in the altered light, mirroring the dark sky in long, metallic-looking slivers against the golden dirt.

Laurel lights a cigarette, drops the match between her knees, and then turns on the radio. It splutters, precisely synchronized with the pickup rocking through a low, rough section . . . this one so bad that their warm meaty shoulders jar together and their heads nod sleepily in the cigarette smoke and the daze of the moment. Then there is music on the radio, coming in louder and brighter than she wanted, so Laurel turns it down a little, and then back up, for the signal fades and wobbles, and then she turns to another station, one that is nearer, with a more stable signal. It is Faron Young singing "Goin' Steady," and J. Dan identifies it for them and spits out the window again. He doesn't seem to be quite as sleepy now, although his eyes are more wrinkled and old-looking, as if he's aged ten years on the journey back.

The music is interrupted by the voice of the disc jockey, who says, "We've had several people call in about the weather, and the only report I can make is, we've received no sky-warning bulletins whatsoever. And there's no indication that tornadoes are forming in any area within two hundred miles."

The music pulses back, and then recedes again briefly as the disc jockey says, "And I mean if it's any farther away than that, Alice, who cares?"

J. Dan turns the radio off, and Laurel says, in an awed voice, "God, can't you just *feel* the air? I mean, really *feel* it! I don't care *what* he says. This is even worse than before! I know it!"

J. Dan nods, but doesn't say anything. Laurel puts her thumb and forefinger before her eye and looks almost cross-eyed at them as she makes quick little feeling motions. The truck lurches through a hole, and a thick cluster of hair falls across her eye. She shakes it back and sighs. "I can *taste* it. I don't care *what* they say. I've been in them before, and there's absolutely nothing like the feel of the air, and the taste, and smell, and everything. As unmistakable as sugar or onions."

"Well, well," Jeffrey says. "What'll we do if it comes? Get off and wave at it. Or maybe eat it. You know, like in big bites?"

"You wouldn't joke about it if you'd ever seen one," Laurel says. "You couldn't believe it. I was in one, when we lived southwest of Wellington for a year when I was about nine. After it was over I saw this broomstick driven into the trunk of a tree, like a big peg. I mean, *fantastic!* You have no *idea!* They even found a cat torn apart in a neighbor's driveway. It had belonged to an old woman on a farm three miles southeast of Wellington. I had nightmares for two years after that. Listen: whatever they say about tornadoes, there's only one thing to consider: if it's un- believable, you know it's true."

J. Dan eases the battered old pickup into low gear, and they start to ascend an incline that seems to drop off into the sky a hundred yards ahead. It has gotten darker, and suddenly they seem to be at the bottom of an enormous pit of black sky. The sun is turning brown.

"Oh God," Laurel groans, "I think I know what it is. J. Dan, it's forming, isn't it? I mean, it's forming right here, all around us, or right overhead. That's why they don't have any weather reports about its coming this way . . . *this* is where the thing's *forming,* right up above!"

"Don't get hysterical," Jeffrey says. "J. Dan, tell her she's full of shit."

"No," J. Dan says, shaking his head back and forth, and easing the car into high gear again, "I won't tell her that, because she's probably just about one-hundred-per-cent right. That is exactly what is happening, if you ask me. It is beginning to rev up its damn engines, right up there in the sky."

For an instant, all three of them are silent as the pickup's gears whine, driving the wheels through a soft area in the road. On both sides, as far as they can see, there is now a deep, bottle-green light in the air, with a dull glow all around them at the rim of the horizon. The sun is suddenly invisible. Overhead, the clouds are as black as midnight.

J. Dan stops the truck and turns off the engine.

"What are you going to do now?" Laurel asks.

"I just want to listen to this here thing," J. Dan says. After the constant drone of the engine, the silence once again seems to smack against their ears. J. Dan opens the door and gets out.

The air drags over them like a tide of muddy water.

"Oh, I knew it," Laurel whispers. "God, I could tell!"

"Is it really a tornado?" Jeffrey asks.

"You better believe it," she says, clutching her hands together and closing her eyes. Then she calls out tensely, "Come back, J. Dan, and for God's sake get us out of here!"

J. Dan is standing round-shouldered at the edge of the road, his Stetson pushed back on his head, and he is gazing all around.

When he comes back to the pickup and gets in, Laurel says, "This is it, isn't it?"

"It sure does damn well *look* like it!" J. Dan says, turning the ignition key and starting the truck once again.

They drive fast for another minute, hoping to get out from under it, but suddenly the light pulses with dust, as if from some giant silent explosion all about them, and the air turns a dull gold. Now the air seems unnaturally thin, and about to ring out with sound. Several raindrops, as big as ripe grapes, burst upon the hood. Then there is a great humming sound overhead.

"Jesus, crazy!" Jeffrey yells, aiming his camera at the windshield.

"All right," J. Dan says. "Let's get the hell out!"

Jeffrey keeps shooting, and J. Dan reaches across Laurel's stomach and jams the door handle down, swinging it open.

"Dive in the damn ditch!" he shouts. "And keep low."

Jeffrey is now standing in the open door, half in and half out of the pickup, still shooting film. Laurel is sitting there with her hands and hair both over her face, paralyzed with fear.

"Get the hell *out!*" J. Dan yells. "It'll take this truck and flip it like a damn beer can! Now get the hell out before I *kick* you out."

There is a sudden banging on the roof and hood of the pickup, and for an instant they watch as hail bounces before their eyes, rattling and skidding off the hood; then the hail stops as suddenly as it started, and they can hear a distant roaring, as if from enormous electric generators starting up over their heads.

The pickup bucks and dances sideways. The blast is tremendous, deafening, hurting their heads and necks and even shoulders with its violence. Great splats of mud are splashing on the hood in an irregular pulse of light, and then the darkness is almost complete, except for a dim haze ringing them, dividing the heavens from the earth.

J. Dan reaches over and kicks the boy out of sight, then shoves Laurel ahead of him and skids across the seat. He's got her around the waist, and dives forward into the blackness, as she starts to scramble in terror.

When they hit the mud, a knee slants across Laurel's mouth, bruising her lips. There is an enormous pounding sound and then a brief ricochet of objects, like the whine of bullets or the sound of exploding buttons, rings, pennies, and teeth.

There is an unfocused cry, total blackness and turmoil, and Laurel gropes against a man's body and hugs it with all her strength, her ear pressed against a thick, strong waist. Even in this blackness she knows it is J. Dan she has grabbed.

The roar is now directly above them. The earth itself seems to shake and drum, and water is pouring heavily over them. For a few seconds the breath is taken out of her, and her arms lose their strength. J. Dan is now holding her against his chest, almost smothering her, his hold is so tight, and she feels her arms push vaguely at him, like those of a drowning swimmer.

But in all this, she remains aloof, as if she is half dreaming it and knows she can wake up if she wants to hard enough.

Her ears start to ring wildly, the drumming is suddenly remote, and an awful silence begins to grow out of the earth, precisely as the light begins to come back. There is no wind at all. Jeffrey is lying on one elbow, staring at her stupidly. Then he shakes his head and says, "Wow!" And shakes it again.

She wants to ask if his ears are ringing, but she doesn't say anything. J. Dan slowly climbs to his feet, like a man with a great load on his back, and puts his Stetson on, closing his eyes as he does so. They are all soaked, and water is gurgling somewhere nearby. Several hailstones the size of marbles are glistening in the mud, but there aren't many. The pickup hasn't moved an inch. They could have stayed inside and remained safe and dry.

"Well, it looks like we made it," J. Dan says. He staggers and then starts to tuck his shirt in. He doesn't look at either of them ... doesn't even ask if they're all right.

"My camera!" Jeffrey says, and goes to the pickup. "I dropped it on the seat."

"Is it all right?" Laurel asks, standing up and trembling all over.

Jeffrey pulls it out and looks at it. Then he holds it to his eye and begins taking footage of Laurel, who closes her eyes and pulls her hair out of her face when she sees what he's doing.

"It looks like maybe it is," J. Dan says. Then he goes to the other door of the pickup, opens it, and fumbles around the glove compartment.

"God, I can't believe it!" Laurel says. She climbs, slipping, to the top of the bank and looks for the cloud, and sees it to the northeast—a great inverted floor of black, more solid than the land. Two towering wisps trail mistily behind like slow, numb flagella.

Then the air around her suddenly brightens, and she looks to the south and sees a rainbow vaulting in huge, silent majesty over the vast undulations of the plains.

"Jeffrey," she cries, "you've got to get this! I mean, I know you don't like color effects, but Christ, you've got to *see* this!"

Jeffrey climbs up beside her and looks, and then says, "It's nice sweet candy, but I've got black and white in here. It wouldn't even show, even if I did want it."

"But you can get the clouds!" Laurel cries, pivoting. "Quick. Look at it retreating over there!"

Jeffrey turns and says, "God, yes!" Then he starts taking pictures of the great shelf of blackness that now seems to be over the town of Maxton, or at least near it.

"It's like now we're in the land of Oz," Laurel says, pulling her hair back and lifting her chin. Her gaze is suddenly dreamy.

"God, it's perfect," Jeffrey whispers. The funnels are gliding together in two enormous parentheses before their eyes—silent, distant, and awesome in their slow, tragic dance. As Laurel watches and Jeffrey films, one of the funnels begins to fade out, and then disappears entirely, leaving the other in sullen isolation.

"It must have hit the town!" Laurel says. "Isn't that where it is?"

"Somewhere over there," Jeffrey answers.

"Maybe it was *killing* people right at that instant . . . right when you were taking footage, and I was watching it. Maybe even right now. One of them is still going. Like *forever*, you know?"

Jeffrey is buried in the scene, intent upon it in a way that few people could understand. As he is always saying, you become part of the camera. Yes, she understands this. The important things are transformed, and then allowed to happen again, inside the camera, upon the turning film.

And then, while the camera is still humming gently, she turns her head and glances down at J. Dan, who is leaning against the fender of the pickup, his eyes closed, drinking from the pint bottle of Old Charter bourbon.

When Jeffrey stops shooting, she lifts a strand of hair out of her face, and then starts to tremble. "My God," she says, "it really did! I mean, it really started right up over us!"

"Like the finger of God pointing straight down," Jeffrey says.

"Don't *talk* like that!" Laurel cries, shuddering.

"It *is* cold," Jeffrey says.

"It's not the cold."

"No, but it's colder than it was."

81

They both pause and look down at J. Dan, who is still leaning against the fender of the pickup, holding the pint bottle up beside his head, as if it were a transistor radio, and staring out of dull, half-closed eyes at the bank before him.

21 "J. Dan," Jeffrey said, "you win, man."

They were approaching Route 70, and sat together in a smell of wet clothes and body heat. J. Dan was stinking of whiskey and animal fatigue. Guiding with his elbows, he dipped a wad of shag out of the pouch and into his mouth. His jaw bulged, and the odor of tobacco was now added to the others. His eyes sagged blearily, and his head nodded slowly back and forth, almost like that of a cyclist pumping, although he was nodding in obscure recognition, not from fatigue.

"*Now* what's he talking about?" he mumbled.

"You're going to wreck us, J. Dan," Laurel said.

"Let me drive," Jeffrey said. "I mean, I understand what you've been saying about Laurel going back to say good-by, and . . . well, I mean, it's like *beautiful*, man!"

"Go fuck a jack rabbit," J. Dan said.

"No, I really mean it. Look, let me drive, will you? I give you my word, *no more stops!* Absolutely."

"Your word isn't worth a pound of shit," J. Dan said.

"Listen, I'm serious now. The way you're going, we'll never get there. I mean, you're not doing over forty, and if you go off the road, man, the whole trip's ended. You know what I mean?"

J. Dan took a deep breath and exhaled. "You touch this damn steering wheel and I will sure as hell bust your damn head open for you."

"Look," Jeffrey said, frowning out the window. "I mean, I can understand how, I mean like *why* you wouldn't trust me. Well,

I'll tell you something. I'll tell you why you *can* trust me when I say I want to get there as much as you do. Okay?"

"Don't," Laurel said. Then she whispered something to him.

"What are you two up to now?" J. Dan said. The pickup weaved slowly to the side, the right wheels sank into the soft shoulder and almost went down. But the pickup whirred and spit mud, and dug its way back onto the gravel.

"That was close," J. Dan said. "But I'll tell you something: I'm getting you there if it's the last thing I do. I promised your mother, and this is one promise, by God, I am not going to break. I owe her this. Time is running out, and it is about time I do something decent in my life, something for somebody else, because a man can't live for himself alone. Not *forever*, he can't. Your shitheaded friend over there would never understand that in a hundred damn years."

After an instant's silence, Laurel said, "Jeffrey just happens to be one of the most idealistic, most imaginative, most selfless people I have ever met."

"You haven't met many people worth anything, then," J. Dan said.

"You don't understand him, J. Dan. And you don't have any right to judge . . . any more right than you have to drag us along with you because of some guilt hang-up, or whatever it is. As for Mother, she has to be filled up with drugs now, and you damned well know it, and she wouldn't know me if she saw me. Her life's over, and there's no point in trying to cover it up with a lot of this sickening sentimental shit. Especially something I don't like *really feel inside*, which would just be dishonest and untrue to my deepest feelings."

"I'm going to explain," Jeffrey said.

"No, don't," Laurel said. She turned to him once more and spoke softly, rapidly, to him, so J. Dan couldn't hear.

"Look," Jeffrey said, raising his voice, "I want to get there. Things have *changed*. I want to get there in *time!*"

J. Dan glanced over and nodded. "He sure is a good actor,"

he said. "And if I didn't already know too much about him, I would be tempted to turn the pickup over to him. Because I have never been so damn tired in my whole life."

"Not to mention a little bit bombed," Laurel said.

"Sometimes a man needs something to help him along a little." J. Dan shifted his wad from his cheek, opened the window, and spat.

"You've had so much help, it's a wonder you can operate at all," Laurel said.

"Shut up. What do *you* know about anything?"

"I know everything. Because I'm Dorothy and the Wizard of Oz is a woman, or maybe that's one of the witches we're going to. I don't know which one, the wicked witch of the west or east or whatever, or the good fairy. Yes, that's what it is, because I don't like that idea of the Wizard in drag."

"I think something hit you over the damn head back there," J. Dan said slowly, shaking his own head.

"I want to get there," Jeffrey said, "because it's part of the whole thing, part of the evolving conception. You know what I mean? It's *got* to become part of it. I mean, it's *got to be*."

"What's he talking about now?" J. Dan asked.

"He's talking about Mother," Laurel said. "He wants to have shots of her at the end. And us, too."

"He *what?*" J. Dan cried.

"I told you we shouldn't have told him," Laurel said rapidly, shaking her hair out of her eyes and gazing at the distance.

"Jesus Christ, but I can't *believe* it!" J. Dan cried. "And you're going to let him *do* something like that?"

"Listen," Laurel said through gritted teeth and still staring in front of her, "he's a brilliant, creative man, an *artist*. Can't you grasp at least *something* of what that like *means*?"

J. Dan slammed on the brakes, making the pickup skid sideways in the gravel, the rear wheels arcing around into the soft mud of the shoulder, striated with sand. He lurched across Laurel's breast and grabbed Jeffrey's collar. Both Laurel and Jeffrey raised their arms to ward off his attack, but J. Dan slammed his fist through them several times, knocking them away, and managing once to hit the side of Jeffrey's head with his fist, only half solidly, but banging it against the window.

Laurel was screaming, and then trying to hang on to J. Dan's upper arms, and panting, wild-eyed, in his face. He could smell her warm puppy breath and see the hatred and fear in her eyes.

The opposite door had been opened, and Jeffrey stood in the mud, holding his camera at his side, and saying, "For Christ's sake, man, what do you think you're *doing?*"

Laurel was still screaming and trying to hold on to J. Dan, but he jerked away from her and got out of the pickup. His legs were rubbery from both drink and fatigue and he could hardly stand up, but he staggered around to the rear of the pickup and then stepped into mud over his ankles, and fell forward heavily onto his elbows, feeling the cold sandy mud clasp his forearms; and then he heard the sound of the camera going in the silence, and J. Dan started to snore, still half awake, with his head bobbing like something encased in lead. Then he let it fall into the mud, not giving a damn, not even able to.

For an instant he lay in the mud; then he struggled to his knees and lurched over onto the gravel and lay back on one elbow.

He saw the pickup tilted to the side, and he knew immediately that the damn thing was stuck. He saw the two silhouettes of Laurel and Jeffrey, outlined against the evening sun. He felt the cold wind chilling his body, but the sensation was distant and muted, like harsh noises in a far room.

Then he rolled over on his back, still in the mud, and, with a thousand damn things falling in slow motion through his mind, passed out.

For an instant, they just stood there and looked at him, and then they came up and jostled his shoulder, calling out to him in low, tense voices. But they couldn't wake him up; so finally, after great effort, they managed to carry him up on the bank and lay him down in the weeds and wild grass, where he'd be more comfortable for a few minutes than if he were cramped up in the seat of the pickup or lying there in the cold gravel.

When he stood up, Jeffrey looked all around.

"Can you see the highway?" Laurel asked, still panting from the effort of helping to carry J. Dan's heavy body; she was standing up and looking, too. Her voice was hushed, a little awed.

"No," Jeffrey said. "Not only that, I think we're probably stuck."

"I know," Laurel said. "He must really be tired. And drunk. Do you suppose he's *all right?*"

Jeffrey stared down at J. Dan for an instant, thinking, and then nodded.

"Aren't you going to try to get it out?" Laurel asked.

"Yes," Jeffrey said. "Because, I mean, I really want to get there. And, like J. Dan keeps saying, time is running out."

"That isn't what he means, and you know it," Laurel said dully.

"Tell me what he means, then?"

"I don't know, but it isn't that."

Jeffrey nodded and then they both climbed down the bank to the pickup, and Jeffrey said, "I'll try to get it out onto the gravel, and then we'll carry him back and put him in. He's more comfortable where he is."

"Do you suppose he's all right?"

"Sure, he's just passed out."

Laurel didn't say anything, so Jeffrey climbed up and started the engine. Laurel stood back and watched him as he rocked the pickup back and forth and spun the tires until they whirred like electric motors, kicking wet mud and sand like clots of brown sugar back against the bank.

J. Dan slept through it all, snoring and utterly limp. Ten minutes later, when Jeffrey gave up trying to get the pickup out, they came back and found him exactly as they had left him, lying absolutely inert on his back, his mouth slightly open and his eyes shut.

"There ought to be somebody coming along," Laurel said. "They could give us a push or something, couldn't they?"

"Maybe," Jeffrey said.

He walked fifteen or twenty feet from J. Dan's sleeping body and gazed directly down upon the pickup. "Betty Bump has let us down," he said.

"We shouldn't have come, and you know it," Laurel said resentfully. "God, I'll never get my head together after this."

"It was essential."

"No it wasn't. Don't talk shit, because I've heard enough! And I want to get into some dry clothes. Take a bath or something. I'm miserable. I'm cold. And J. Dan might catch cold or pneumonia or something. He looks horrible, and I mean, his resistance *has* to be low."

"J. Damn is indestructible," Jeffrey said in a low voice.

"Nobody's *that*," Laurel said. "Not even J. Dan. And don't call him that."

"All right, but J. Dan is. And I'm going to get everything. Everything about him. I'm going to get your mother, because she's the Holy Grail, you know what I mean? The quest motif. The whole bit. I'm serious."

"You're a little bit crazy, maybe," Laurel said. "And I'm getting awfully fucking cold. It's getting dark, and if somebody doesn't come by, what are we going to do?"

"There'll be somebody coming by," Jeffrey said.

"You don't know how godforsaken some of these places are," Laurel said. "If you did, you wouldn't be so confident."

"Tell me something: what's his reason? I mean, he keeps talking about doing something decent in his life for a change, or whatever. What's he done that's so bad?"

"Nothing that I ever knew of," Laurel said. "I mean, he couldn't settle down with his first marriage, and I guess he's done his share of whoring and drinking and things like that. But I don't think that has anything to do with it. If you want my opinion, I think he fell on his fucking head too many times when he was a rodeo clown."

Jeffrey nodded and thought for a moment. Then he slid down the bank and climbed up into the pickup. Without looking back at Laurel, he picked up his notebook and started printing. Laurel watched him for a while, and then went back and stood over J. Dan, staring out at the darkening sky.

22

VECTORS OF P.M. SUNLIGHT CONTRA CIRCULAR MOTIF. OR VECTOR OF AFTERNOON SHADOWS. LIGHT & DARK. GENIUS OF BLACK AND WHITE IS ESSENTIALLY MANICHEAN (MANICHEAN MANIKINS).

CF. DEF. OF CINEMA AS "OPTICAL PUN": OK, BUT MORE THAN THIS. THE FRAME IS CELL OF THE FILM (EISENSTEIN): BUT ALSO MICROCOSM OF THE FILM. ERGO, THE FILM IS THE ACT OF VANISHING. THE SYMBOL EVAPORATES WASHES CLEAR (THIS ITS "SOLUTION") THE INSTANT IT EXISTS (LIKE SOUND: CF. ONG & MCLUHAN). IT STRIVES TO PERPETUATE ITSELF IN THE ACT OF VANISHING, AGAINST THE ONSLAUGHT OF ITS OWN LIKENESS, SIMULACRUM (THE SUCCEEDING FRAME), AND THUS ALLEGORIZES HUMAN LIFE ITSELF IN ITS CONTINUOUS, TERRIBLE, DANCING MOTION. OR THE CEREMONY OF EVANESCENCE.

AND AS IT IS WITH THE FRAME, SO IS IT WITH THE MACROCOSM, THE TOTAL FILM AS STATEMENT.

LIKE FELLINI'S "NEO-REALISM" AN EVASIVE FORMULA. WHY? ALSO HIS BELIEF THAT EVERY INVESTIGATION IS SPIRITUAL (HIS FILMS THIS). BUT HIS ALEATORY APPROACH CORRECT. FELLINI SAYS HE'S LUCKY. LIKE GENIUS IS LUCKY: TO HAVE LUCK IS GENIUS.

BUT WHAT ABOUT HIS IDEA OF FILM AS CONFESSIONAL? CINEMA AS TRUEST MEDIUM OF MAGIC? DIRECTOR AS THAUMATURGE?

NO, MY IDEA OF EVENTION GETS NEARER THE HEART. I CAN
EVEN HEAR THE THUB-DUB. WHY NOT?

EVERYBODY SHOULD MAKE FILM . . . THUS LIVE COUNTERLIFE.
MEDIUM HAS GENIUS: WHICH MEANS CAN'T MISS.

BUT WHAT ABOUT THOSE EQUIPPED WITH GENIUS BEFORE THEY
ENTER THE QUADRILATERAL CAGE OF THE SHOT WITH THEIR MINDS?

LIKE, WHAT IF HENRY JAMES COULD HAVE MADE A FILM?!!
GOD!

THE PARADOX AND COLLISION OF ENERGY FIELDS STUNS THE
MIND.

ALSO FILM CONCERNED WITH APPEARANCE, NOT REALITY. THE
MOVIE THEATER IS PLATO'S CAVE (ALSO LIVING ROOM LIGHTED
BY A TV SET), AND EVERY DAY IT'S HARDER TO SEE THE OUTSIDE
LIGHT. BUT ONE'S AS REAL AS OTHER. WHY NOT? MAN LIVES AS
FULLY IN WHAT HE CREATES AS IN WHAT WAS THERE BEFORE.

SOMEDAY WE MIGHT WATCH OUR LIVES AS THEY ARE LIVED.

AGAIN, WHY NOT?

23 "Do you suppose he's *all right,* lying back there? Don't
you think we ought to get him back into the truck?"

Jeffrey punched his ball-point pen and stuck it back in his
pocket. He looked out at Laurel as she stood in the mud and
sand and stared back at him earnestly. The wind was blowing
her hair across her forehead, and her face was dark from the
evening.

"Maybe you're right," Jeffrey said. He got out of the pickup
and stood beside her. The wind smelled sour and a little wild, as
if from rotting vegetation.

"I mean, it's getting *cold,*" Laurel said, shivering all over. She
looked back in the direction of J. Dan.

"You can't see him from the road," Jeffrey said. "Let's just leave him there for a while longer. If somebody comes by to pull us out, I don't want them seeing him like that. I mean, covered all over with mud and everything, and we can't even bring him around. I don't want anything to keep us from getting there on time."

"Yes, but do you suppose he's all *right?*" Laurel cried.

"What I don't want is some shithead trying to help us," Jeffrey said. "I mean, think there's something wrong with him, or we hit him over the head and are stealing his pickup, or something. I know that sounds crazy, but remember the way they looked us over back there in that town. And everybody's bound to be up tight after what we just went through. Like, maybe . . ."

"Yes, but you could just say he was drunk, or something, which is the truth, and he fell in the mud and passed out."

Jeffrey grabbed her arm and said, "It's too late for that. Here comes a car, now."

She looked ahead and saw it coming, and saw that its headlights were on even though the sky was still somewhat light. The breeze blew harder and made her shiver again.

"We'll come back and get him the minute the pickup's free and whoever it is has pulled us out and gone his way."

"All right," she said, "but I wish we'd gotten him back into the car. I don't feel right about it."

They both went down into the road and watched as a dusty and splattered green station wagon crept toward them, its headlights pulsing bright and dim as the car worked its way cautiously over the uneven road. Both of them stood there waiting, and when the car coasted to a stop before them, they saw a tanned, middle-aged man open the door and get out. He was wearing a gray flannel shirt and a Stetson, which he fastened on his head when he got out.

Jeffrey nudged Laurel with his elbow, and said, "Look! I can't believe it. Another J. Dan!"

"No," she said ambiguously, but there was no opportunity to clarify what she meant, because the man was walking toward them and saying, "Well, it looks like maybe you're in some trouble."

"We sure are," Jeffrey said.

"I've got me a tow chain in back, and I think maybe I can pull you out," the man said.

Then he walked up to the pickup and put his foot on the front bumper. "Were you two in the twister that just now hit Maxton?"

"We sure were," Jeffrey said. "Our clothes are still wet."

The man nodded. "I'm going up there to help out if I can. It was really bad. Tore up the place, and they don't know how many were killed. The damn thing went on and just missed Wakeeny. Jumped right over the town."

"That's really something," Jeffrey said.

"Sounds like the worst they've *ever* had around here," the man said, shaking his head. He stared thoughtfully at the pickup for a few seconds, and then took his foot down from the bumper and looked first at Laurel and then at Jeffrey.

"You two from around here?" he said.

"No, we're from Colorado," Jeffrey said.

The man nodded. "Yeah, I guess I could tell that from the license plate. What you doing on a little bitty road like this?"

"We were taking a short cut from Maxton," Jeffrey said. "We were headed back to Route 70 and got stuck."

The man snorted. "Some short cut!"

"Actually, we got sort of lost," Jeffrey said.

"Yeah, looks like it."

"We're really in sort of a hurry," Laurel said. "I mean, my mother's very sick . . . in fact, she's dying and we're trying to get to her. She's in Colorado."

"Whereabouts in Colorado?" the man said.

"It's a ranch in Meeker County," Laurel said.

The man nodded. "Well, I'll see if I can get you out of that hole you're in." He turned to Jeffrey. "Tell you what: I'll drive on up behind your pickup and fasten my log chain to your rear bumper and see if I can't pull you out backward. That way, we won't have to pass each other, because that's a problem on *this* road. Then you can go your way, and I can go mine. Okay?"

"Sounds fine," Jeffrey said.

"You just put her in reverse and ease gently on the gas. Don't spin your wheels, but just keep easing it when I start rocking her backward. We should have her out of there in a jiffy."

"Okay," Jeffrey said.

The man got into his station wagon and drove it forward until its rear was just beyond the pickup's, and then stopped, letting the engine idle. Laurel hugged herself and shivered as she watched the exhaust vapors curl up past the shining red tail lights of the station wagon.

The man opened the back of the wagon, dragged out a heavy log chain, and hooked it loosely over the rear bumper of the pickup. Then he stood in almost the identical place where J. Dan had lain only a short while ago, and checked it out to see if it was okay.

He nodded to Jeffrey, and Jeffrey started the engine of the pickup. Laurel turned and looked up at the bank where J. Dan was lying, hidden in the grass and weeds.

"Aren't you going to get in?" the man asked.

Laurel glanced at him and nodded, and then holding her hands up beside her shoulders, made her way gingerly along the mud rim of the road to the pickup.

"Okay," Jeffrey called, waving his arm out the window.

The man started the wagon and began to rock the pickup slowly backward.

Jeffrey started to spin the wheels, but then the left rear wheel caught in the gravel and spit a little until the back of the pickup was on the road.

He got out and thanked the man as he unhooked the log chain. Then they both got back into their cars, and Jeffrey sat there racing the engine until the man started to drive slowly away.

"We better go on a few hundred yards," Jeffrey said, easing the pickup forward. "Because that old cat is suspicious."

"Two *hippies*," Laurel said in her old-lady voice, "driving a *rancher's* truck!"

"That's about right," Jeffrey said.

"Only don't go too far," Laurel said. "Because we want to get him."

"I wouldn't forget him for anything," Jeffrey said.

They started going a little faster, and sure enough, looking in his rear-vision mirror, Jeffrey could see the station wagon almost stopped on the next swell, looking for the pickup . . . the old cat suspicious as hell, wondering what they would be lingering here for . . . probably wondering why two people like them would be driving a rancher's pickup in the first place.

"He thinks we stole it or something," Jeffrey said.

"In a way we did," Laurel said.

"Well, I'll keep going until that old son of a bitch is satisfied."

"I only hope we can find the place when we come back."

"It'll be easy," Jeffrey said. "We can see where the wheel tracks are in the mud."

"Yes, but it's almost dark. I've never seen it get dark so fast as it does out here. That's one reason I'm sorry I ever came back. That and the windmills. I don't know what it is, but there's something about them that just scares the *shit* out of me!"

"It's only for a short while," Jeffrey said, "and anyway, it's got to be."

They drove silently for a few seconds, and then Laurel said, "Aren't you going to go back and get him?"

"I'm looking for a place to turn around. I don't want to get stuck again. I mean, there isn't any *room!*"

"You could back up," Laurel said. "It isn't that far."

"No, but it's kind of dark. I don't want to go off the road again. It's hard backing that far in the dark."

"Go on, there are backup lights on it."

"Are you sure? Betty Bump has seen her best days."

But he stopped anyway, and shifted into reverse. "I only hope our good Samaritan has gone," he said.

"Oh, he's gone by now. He's gone Samaritaning in Maxton."

Jeffrey opened the door and began to drive backward up and down over the muddy gravel road. They went like this for a while, and then he said, "Keep looking on that side. That's where the wheel tracks will be."

"Don't worry," she shouted. "I'm looking."

Then it was he saw another car approaching from the rear. The headlights appeared briefly on a swell, and then silently and abruptly disappeared behind one of the dark undulations of the land.

He stopped and told her, and Laurel said, "What will we do?"

Jeffrey took a deep breath and said, "Well, we're going to have to keep on going for a while, until we pass a side road. There's no passing on *this* damn part."

"We shouldn't have left him," Laurel said. "My God, it's like things are getting out of control! We don't even know what we're doing!"

Jeffrey watched the headlights appear once more in the rear-vision mirror and then sink into the darkness. "They're about two hills behind," he said. "And I'd better start moving or they'll get suspicious." He started the pickup forward.

"I don't get it," Laurel said. "I mean it's all so perfectly fucking *innocent*, and here we are acting like we're *criminals* or something. I mean, it's *unreal!*"

"We're aliens in an unfriendly land, when you come right down to it," Jeffrey said. "Isn't that what you've been saying all along? Isn't that why you left in the first place?"

"I don't know what you're saying," Laurel said, shaking her head violently.

The car soon caught up with them, and followed them as if tethered to forty feet of rope.

"There's got to be a damn turnoff somewhere," Jeffrey said.

"The farther we go," Laurel said, "the harder it's going to be to *find* him. Haven't you thought of that?"

"Look, don't get hysterical. Okay?"

"That's another pickup back there," Laurel said.

"I noticed."

In a few minutes, however, they came to a lonely crossroad, and Laurel sighed in relief. Jeffrey turned the pickup to the right, and the pickup behind roared away past them, straight ahead, splattering mud, stones, and sand.

Jeffrey backed up, turned the pickup around, and started back.

"Look out for the tracks," she said.

"Don't worry," Jeffrey said. "There can't be too many of them."

They drove in tense silence for a few minutes, and finally Laurel said, "Are you sure we haven't passed it? I mean, it's so *dark!*"

"I don't think so," Jeffrey said. "But we've got to be getting near."

"Christ," she said, "it all looks alike."

Then, when the headlights began to rise after the pickup's descent into one of the shallow declivities, they saw the smeared gravel, and the deep tracks emerging from the striated mud of the shoulder.

"This is it," she said, and Jeffrey stopped the pickup.

They both got out, leaving the engine running and the lights on, and climbed up the bank.

The wind had risen, and by now it was dark. On the distant horizon to the northeast, they could see a sprinkling of lights. And to the west, there was the glowing rim of the earth. A few stars were out. Elsewhere, it was almost black. They could see a little, however, because they were standing in long, deep shadows from the headlights of the pickup. A few stars were out.

"I can't find him," Laurel said in a hushed voice.

"He's got to be here somewhere," Jeffrey said.

"But he's *not!* We'd *see* him if he *were here,* wouldn't we?"

"I don't know," Jeffrey said stupidly. "Are you sure this is the place? I mean, couldn't those be *other* tire tracks? You know, from somebody else going over into the mud?"

"Oh, Christ!" Laurel whispered. "We shouldn't have left him."

"What are you talking about? He couldn't have gotten up! And nobody's going to steal his *body,* for Christ's sake!"

"I'm afraid he was really like *sick* or something."

"Look, don't be hysterical. We couldn't even wake him up *ourselves.* Remember?"

"Yes, but *something* must have happened. I mean, he's *just not here!*"

"I know it, I know it," Jeffrey said rapidly, in a low, tense voice. For a few seconds they thrashed around in the grass and weeds, and then Jeffrey said, "I mean, if we only had a flashlight. Didn't he keep one in the glove compartment?"

"I'll go look," Laurel said, sliding down off the bank toward the lighted pickup, still idling in the middle of the road.

Jeffrey paced back and forth along the bank until she returned, shining a flashlight in his face.

"Don't shine it in my eyes, you'll blind me," he said.

Both of their voices had gotten still lower, as if they didn't want to be heard. The wind pushed insistently and brainlessly at them, and they were both chilled and tired.

"We've *got* to find him," Laurel said.

"Look, will you please shut up and help me look?" Jeffrey said. "He's got to be here someplace. If not, we'll go back farther. He's either around here, close by . . . like maybe he's come awake or something, and staggered a little way off . . . or else we've stopped at the wrong place. In which case, we don't panic, but simply get in the pickup and back up some more until we find more wheelprints in the damn mud."

"God, I only hope you know what you're doing," Laurel said. "But I feel sick. I only wish we'd never started this whole fucking business. I mean, Jeffrey, I'm really *scared*, you know?"

They were looking at each other briefly when they heard the horn of the pickup blow, so close to them and so loud that they jumped almost simultaneously.

"He's in the pickup!" Laurel cried. She started skidding down the bank, with Jeffrey following.

When they came past the headlights, they saw that the doors were both closed, and no one was visible inside.

"Let me open it," Jeffrey said, reaching around Laurel and working the handle of the door. It came open, turning the light on inside and showing J. Dan lying half on the seat and half on the floor, with his rifle in his hand.

He lifted his dark and drunken face toward them and said in a dull, hoarse voice, "Don't try it again or I kill you."

But he was far gone, and Jeffrey simply pulled the rifle from his fingers and lifted him to a sitting position against the door on the right side.

"Lock the door," Laurel said, "or he'll fall out."

"Okay, it's locked. Come on and get in beside him. I'll drive."

He crawled out and Laurel got in. Then Jeffrey climbed up in the driver's seat and started forward.

"There's a wide place in the road up here, if I remember right," he said slowly. "I'm going to give it a try, anyway."

Laurel didn't say anything, but when they had gone about a mile, she buried her face in both hands. J. Dan was lying collapsed against the door, breathing heavily.

When Jeffrey found the wide place in the road, he said out loud, "Well, it *looks* firm, and I'm going to try it."

"Go ahead," Laurel said distantly, without removing her face from her hands.

Jeffrey managed to turn the pickup around, and when he started accelerating again, Laurel lifted her face and said, "J. Dan, are you all right?"

"He can't hear you," Jeffrey said.

"I'll make it," J. Dan said, without opening his eyes.

The pickup jarred their shoulders warmly together when it hit the stony bottom between swells; and then when it began to climb again, its headlights probing dully at the night sky, Jeffrey said, "J. Dan, how did you manage to move after we'd tried as hard as we could to wake you up?"

There was a pause, and then, with his eyes still closed, J. Dan said, "I had me a nightmare, sonny boy. Only part of it is still with me. I woke up and stumbled down the bank, and then I went along the road a ways, and then I saw the pickup coming back."

Jeffrey nodded slowly, but didn't say anything.

About twenty minutes later, they came upon Route 70, and Laurel said, "I don't care what you say, we ought to stop at a motel and take a shower and let him get some decent rest, like in a bed, and sober up."

"Christ, I'm tired too," Jeffrey said.

"And maybe you think I'm not," Laurel said. There were tears in her eyes as she lighted a cigarette.

In less than an hour, they had turned off Route 70 again, and had checked in at the Western View Motel, at one edge of a little town named Shields.

They had to help J. Dan into the room, where they took off his clothes, gave him a shower, and put him to bed.

Then Laurel and Jeffrey themselves took showers, hung up their dirty clothes, and went to bed, where they dreamed separate dreams, as separated from each other as surely as if they had been miles apart and one of them had been dying.

24 Slow-motion, J. Dan swims forward through an empty, darkened room, reaching for the camera and the audience, striving with each pained gesture to obliterate it, his face grotesquely troubled.

He swings his fist, and then falls sideways; but catches himself, and in slow-motion outrage pulls around to face the audience again, and then gathers his strength and comes lurching forward, with every lineament of murderous intent upon his face.

Suddenly the room has changed, and there is J. Dan standing motionless at the top of the stairs. There is nothing in the house but darkness. He stares downward, and then, after a stop-motion, as if he's arrested in the act of hearing the beginning drumbeat (pulse/time), he is plunging down the stairs, his mouth open and his hair waving in the muted light, like kelp in a deep and lazy sea.

His stiffened arm lurches toward the railing, and the railing and balusters all splinter slowly, expanding like a time-phase photograph of burgeoning pods, and J. Dan turns in a leisurely arc, a skydiver caught in his fall, the hills and dales beneath flickering in abstract inconsequence, rolling over and forward, toward the hated lens, the voyeurist audience, the ground.

Now there is the house, tilted against a roiled sky. At the corner, there is the windmill, like a ladder that reaches only into air and wind and nothing. The drum beats, the flute plays.

Out of the door, J. Dan comes running, ludicrously slow, ludicrously dark, ludicrously bulky as he wades painfully and nightmarishly toward the lens, seeking to obliterate it with his vestigial fists that extend like dinosaurian weapons from his monstrous arms.

25 Jeffrey awoke first, and lay on his back staring at the still-dark ceiling. J. Dan was snoring heavily, and Laurel lay warmly on her side, naked, facing him and emitting a small, fluttering breath upon his left arm.

The motel room was dark, although Jeffrey knew it was daylight because of the silver rim on the drapes. The room smelled musty; it smelled of sleep and stale whiskey and chewing tobacco and sweat and dirty clothes. It was too warm.

He reached over and turned on the light, and looked at both J. Dan and Laurel. Neither of them moved, so he got out of bed and put on his drawers. He looked at his watch, which said seventwenty, wound it meditatively, and then put it on.

He walked over to the window and reached through the drapes to touch the glass. It was cold. The sky was low, swollen, heavy, and seemed to be threatening rain or snow.

When he turned around, he saw J. Dan looking at him.

"Well," he said. "How are you doing?"

"I don't feel so damn good," J. Dan said. "The time comes when you don't bounce back the way you used to. Time doesn't stop for *no* man."

"That's too bad," Jeffrey said, frowning and shaking his head. For an instant he seemed to be genuinely sympathetic.

J. Dan sat up in bed with his legs over the side and held his head in his hands. "Where are my damn undershorts," he said after a minute.

"They're hanging up on one of the hangers, back by the washbasin," Jeffrey said. He went back, got them, and threw them on the bed. J. Dan stood up and put them on. Then he sat down on the bed again.

He stared at Laurel, who was still sleeping.

"We ought to be getting a start, don't you think?" Jeffrey asked. "I mean, maybe you'd better phone now, if you want to, and then we can get started."

J. Dan looked back at him dully, and then nodded. In her bed Laurel took a swift breath and turned over, raising her arm above her head, so that her soft, heavy breast came out from under the covers.

J. Dan stared at it an instant, and then nodded again. "I'll phone them from the office. Or the restaurant. They got a restaurant here?"

"Sure," Jeffrey said. "But you can call here, now."

"No," J. Dan said. "Three's a crowd. I'll give you two a chance to get yourselves dressed in peace. As soon as I can get dressed. Then we'll have breakfast, as soon as you get there. And get started." He was still sitting on the bed, hunched over and tired-looking.

"Yes, we ought to get started," Jeffrey said. "I mean, you're right, you know?"

"I know," J. Dan said.

Then he noticed that Laurel's eyes were open, and she was looking at him sleepily, her breast still uncovered.

"Hello, J. Dan," she said tonelessly.

"Hello," he said.

She turned over and stared at Jeffrey, but she didn't speak.

J. Dan stood up and went back to the washbasin and, with a trembling hand, turned the water on. He leaned against the basin with his arms straight and his head lowered.

"How do you feel?" she asked from the bed.

"I'd feel a little better if I had me a razor and could shave," he said. "It helps a man to shave and freshen up. A man has to have pride."

Laurel closed her eyes and said, "Yes, it seems to me I've heard the word."

Jeffrey whispered to her, "I don't think he remembers. You know, about my getting like *some footage* when we get there."

Laurel stared at him, but didn't answer. Then she sat up in bed, her breasts hanging heavily, and scratched at her hair.

When J. Dan came back out, he looked at her nakedness for an instant, and said, "Well, I am going to go make the call."

"How far are we?" Jeffrey asked.

"I don't even know where we're at," J. Dan said in a dull, hurt voice.

"It's a town named Shields."

"Then we're almost to the border. We should be there in a couple of hours of driving."

"The border?" Jeffrey asked.

"No, home."

Laurel got out of bed and stretched her stomach toward him, and then recommenced scratching at her scalp.

J. Dan nodded, as if he recognized her nakedness, and then put on his Stetson and went out.

"I wonder if she's still alive," Laurel said, sitting back down on the bed and rounding her shoulders.

"I hope she is," Jeffrey said.

For an instant she stared at him, and then she said, "What sort of shots do you want to get? I mean, your sudden interest in this whole, fucking, drab business truly amazes me."

Jeffrey went to the window and looked out. When he answered her, his voice was muted; he was speaking into the drapes, as if he didn't completely want to be heard. "The interest is there. When things intensify as they have in the past twenty-four hours, there is something deep and vital at the heart of it. You have to get it all down, all on film. You *have* to respect it . . . be like *humble* before it. It's not callous, no matter what you think. Then you look for what it is. But you have to have an instinct to detect the larger shape that keeps the real thing inside it. You like *event* the film, instead of *inventing* it."

"I mean, I've really heard you talk this shit before," Laurel said dreamily, falling back on the bed and throwing her arm over her eyes. "I mean, existence precedes essence, and who the fuck cares?"

"Come on and get dressed," he said. "We can't waste time. We've got to get there. This whole damn thing has got to be."

"I've heard that before, too," Laurel said. But she got up anyway, and thudded barefoot back to the washbasin.

Jeffrey was still looking out the window, staring now at the mud-splattered pickup, Betty Bump.

When she had put on her dirty clothes again, and came up to him at the window, he said, "You were right; we shouldn't have told him about the plans for following through. You know, getting shots of everything, right to the end. Your mother, and all."

"That's an understatement if I ever heard one," Laurel said. "It's a wonder he didn't kill you, or wreck us worse than he did."

Jeffrey nodded. "You were right."

"You know, you're always like *saying* that . . . I mean the bit about other people being right and everything; and you sound generous and liberal-minded as hell, but do you know something? You don't ever deviate one fucking inch from what you've had in mind all along."

Jeffrey turned his head and looked at her without speaking for an instant, and then turned back to the window, still holding the drapes aside.

Laurel lighted a cigarette and exhaled at the back of his neck. "Not that it makes any difference," she said, sitting back on the bed. Then she stood back up and dusted cigarette ashes off her T-shirt.

Jeffrey's voice was dreamy, as if he were preoccupied with something he saw in the sky. "But you know," he said, "he doesn't remember. I mean, I was expecting a lot of shit from him this morning, but not a word. He just doesn't remember."

"It's hard to tell how much he drank yesterday," Laurel said. "And I guess he *was* awfully tired."

"And what sort of nightmare do you suppose he had, lying there in the cold, windy grass, under the stars? When he woke up, he must have thought we'd stolen the pickup."

"If he could think anything."

"Oh, he wasn't that bad off."

"It's hard to tell," Laurel said. She sat down on the bed again, and then lay back and stared at the ceiling. "It must be awfully important for you to make this film," she said. "I only wish I understood it more."

"I keep trying to tell you there's not much to really like *understand* at this stage," Jeffrey said. "Now is when you immerse yourself in the material. And Christ, *what* material! I don't think you can even begin to realize what J. Dan is . . . I mean, how *potent* the old son of a bitch is. Like, what he's doing. The *pietas* he's caught up in, like an epic hero or something. You know?"

"I can't see him that way," Laurel said, "because of what I know about him. I'm sorry, but what you're saying just sounds like so much shit."

"What you know about him is like history, and only one dimension of that . . . so it's really only a construct, a sort of fiction that's useful to you, and you alone; so it can get in the way of other meanings," Jeffrey said. "Like what's really there, alive and waiting."

"Maybe. But why you would want to shoot footage of a dying woman . . . after a lifetime of pampering herself and being a martyr to the ethics of good grooming . . . I mean, the irony is that now she probably won't even be *presentable*, you know? Let alone, photogenic. I mean photogenic even in *your* sense."

"It's all part of the material. It's all part of the truth wanting to be manifest, wanting to be seen. All the world's a screen and to be alive is to want to catch it on the wing."

"That sounds like a mixed metaphor to me," Laurel said, sitting up in the bed and looking at him. "Incidentally, aren't you going to get dressed? So we can like get started?"

Jeffrey nodded. "You're right; we've got to get going. You do understand, don't you?" he said.

Laurel frowned and said, "Sure; I mean, when you come right down to it, she's just another woman. If we have to go there in the first place, I don't give a shit what you do. Crazy or not. Be my guest."

"You're quite a broad, do you know that?" he said.

She smiled distantly and said, "Well, sweet cocksman, why don't you show me, then? You know, like *show, don't tell.*"

Jeffrey shook his head and patted her side. "No, you're dressed, and we have to get moving. I mean, we've got to get there before it's too damn late."

"You're beginning to sound like him," Laurel said.

"Not in a thousand years," Jeffrey said.

"I'm not so sure."

"Well, you can be. Because it's absolutely, totally different. We're running on completely different tracks. Altogether."

"If you say so," Laurel said, putting on her CPO jacket and shaking her hair out of her face.

"What's she like?" Jeffrey asked.

"Who?"

"Your mother. You know, what sort of person is she?"

"You know what she's like. I've told you about her a thousand times."

"Yes, but then I wasn't thinking about her in this way. I mean, she's *different* now. It's almost like I can see her through J. Dan's eyes. Only I want to know more about her."

"See, I was right," Laurel said. "You *are* beginning to sound like him. I mean, it's like you're even *siding* with him against me or something."

"No, I'm not. Listen, back there in the pickup, it was *me* he hit, or was trying to hit, not you!"

"Yes, but that's something different."

"Look, all I asked you was, what's she like?"

"She's what everybody used to call 'a lovely woman,' like I've told you a hundred times. She wears a size nine dress and won't let anybody forget it, and she has fantastic clothes that she buys in Dallas. She *flies* down there about once or twice a year, and we practically live in a shack, you know? And she's crazy about jewelry. J. Dan bought her a pearl necklace that cost over six hundred dollars. *That* kind of shit. Not that she doesn't like *share* or anything; but I mean, *who cares?* And she thinks God uses Palmolive soap and fluoride toothpaste. And when I started getting buck-toothed, at like the age of three, she held it against me *personally*, as if I was a disgrace to her or something, having buckteeth and wearing a size sixteen when I was still in high school. Even when she was forty-five, when I last laid eyes on her, she was still so fucking lovely she could have won the title of 'Miss Middle-Aged Eastern Colorado' or something. And except for this one torrid love affair with that romantic Don Juan, J. Dan Swope, you'd think she was living in 1890 or 1900 or something, because she's still a mid-Victorian, and so fucking moral and hypocritical you couldn't believe it even if I told you. And that's all I'm going to tell you, because I get actually, physically sick when I think about her too much."

Jeffrey nodded.

"Now are you getting the idea?" Laurel asked. "Is it beginning to sink into your head what this whole trip is like *doing* to me?"

"It's ironic," Jeffrey said. "I mean, a beautiful woman grows old, and even if she keeps her beauty, the beauty she keeps is itself eventually dated. You know what I mean? Like, the beauty she once had was okay in 1940 or 1950 or something, but now—even if she had every bit of it intact . . . I mean, it would just be irrelevant. It wouldn't communicate."

"That's exactly it!" Laurel cried, grabbing his arm and shaking it. She tried to catch his eye, but he was slowly shaking his head, and his look was distant.

"It's gotten cold," he said, going to the chair where his CPO lay. "I can tell from the window. And the look of the sky."

Laurel glanced at the two messed-up beds and said, "I'd still rather go back to Wichita. Even this late. I mean, I'm truly sorry we began this whole, fantastic, fucking business. You'll never know."

"Fantastic's the word," Jeffrey said, opening the door and going out.

"I feel like I'm going to puke," Laurel says tentatively, but Jeffrey doesn't pay any attention, even though he didn't close the door and had obviously heard what she'd said.

26 Out of the far holding pen, a man comes riding a bucking Brahman bull, his face pale in the gray, dusty air. He is in slow motion, and when the camera swells the image into close-up, the viewer can see every motion of his jarring body, the wrinkles of his shirt jumping into view, and then vanishing almost as suddenly as his torso straightens out from the previous jolt, and the panicked, monstrous beast that carries him falls once again to the earth, its legs hitting like beams that could hold a house erect, jarring its own and its rider's flesh in the mute and abrupt deceleration, pushing the cowboy's stomach into an accordion of flesh, intestines, wrinkled cloth . . . and then the hand is waving slow-motion time to the leisurely thudding, and the Brahman bull turns suddenly to the side, spilling the cowboy down over its massively pumping shoulder to the earth, where he rolls once and then is crouching, dazed and scared, half turning around without rising farther to watch the damned thing and be ready if it turns back upon him.

There is the muted sound of a crowd blowing noise down out of the crude wooden bleachers, and then the camera zooms in on one of the clowns, his face bearing an enormous grin, like a cup that holds a big cherry nose and two blackberry eyes in abstract design above its rim.

The clown takes three steps forward and closely watches the fallen rider, then flicks a look to the side at the Brahma bull as it turns and begins to trot busily back toward him.

Underneath the clown's bulb nose, the real nose is broken; behind the painted, manic cup of a grin, the mouth is grim.

But he really doesn't mind; and it would be melodramatic to suggest that his job is really all that dangerous, even though this particular Brahma bull is a son of a bitch on hooves, as just about everybody knew when they first ran him into the holding pen.

The cowboy knew it, but he rode him anyway, giving an opportunity for the camera to record the squeeze and expansion of his accordion stomach as he progressed in silence across a dusty arena of light.

And now the clown knows it, as he says (the caption jumps into print at the bottom of the scene), "Well, it has got to be done, and since I am the one in the damn clown suit, I have got to be the one who does it."

So he staggers ludicrously out into the path of the Brahma bull and interrupts him with such a flourish that the bull turns first its head, and then its body aside, so that its course begins to slant, the way a small boat begins to drift sideways and close in toward a dock.

But then there is another clown nearby, one whose expression is woeful, defeated. He takes his turn and diverts the Brahma bull from the first clown. The cowboy escapes, and a caption beneath the first clown says, "If you take the trouble to look, there is usually somebody to give you a hand. Nobody is alone in that damn arena. If they ever are, it is a sad damn world."

The crowd cheers, and then the cheering begins to throb, like the beat of a drum that shakes the shadows, and ripples the darkness of the stands, the Brahma bull, the three isolated figures of men standing in the dust.

27 "Well, she is still hanging on," J. Dan says, standing up when they approach his booth. He sits down again, jarring a half-empty glass of Bromo-Seltzer and the water glasses, and Laurel once more gazes, half hypnotized, at the surfaces of water sliding back and forth. Then she also sits down.

The motel restaurant is small—a dining area packed neatly around a counter, and ringed with half a dozen booths. The waitress, dressed in a too-tight green uniform, is plump, young, and blonde, with an angry red skin. She walks flat-footed up to the table and holds her pad and pencil ready, without saying anything.

"I guess we will order us some breakfast now," J. Dan says in his slow, rough voice, frowning down at the menu with a judicious look.

"Maybe you'll feel better after you eat," Laurel says.

J. Dan nods. "I usually do."

"I just want a glass of orange juice and a bowl of cornflakes," Jeffrey says. He puts his notebook on the table, punches his ball-point pen and starts printing.

"Doing his homework again, I see," J. Dan says.

"I just want a poached egg and toast and coffee," Laurel says, handing her menu to the waitress. The waitress takes it, flicking a slowing look over Laurel, taking in the way she's dressed. Then she shifts her look to J. Dan.

"I think I will have me a couple eggs, over light, a breakfast steak, home fries, and a damn pot of coffee," he says, closing the menu and looking out at the weather.

"Is she really just the same?" Laurel asks, when the waitress leaves.

"No change," J. Dan says.

"Maybe she'll pull through again," Laurel says.

"Not from what they said, she won't. From what they told me, it's a damn wonder she has lasted this long."

"Maybe it's like she's waiting," Jeffrey says, looking up from his notebook.

"Go back to your schoolwork, sonny boy," J. Dan says.

"He's not in school," Laurel says. "He graduated long ago."

"About time he goes to work, it seems to me," J. Dan says.

"Well, at least I'm glad you're feeling better. Last night, you were too far gone to even bitch about us."

"Last night I was in bad shape for *damn* sure!" J. Dan says, shaking his head. He starts to tap his fingers on the tablecloth, looking out at the parking lot. "They say it is going to snow," he says.

"That's all we need," Laurel says, lifting a strand of hair out of her eyes, and staring down at the empty table before her.

"Does your boy friend take pictures all the time?" J. Dan asks conversationally, looking at Jeffrey's notebook.

"It isn't exactly a game," Laurel says. "I mean, Jeffrey has already won two awards with his film making. Haven't you, Jeffrey?"

When Jeffrey doesn't answer, Laurel takes out her own notebook and starts to write the first draft of a poem. When she has completed three lines, she suddenly cries out, "Oh, my God!"

Both Jeffrey and J. Dan look at her, and J. Dan says, "What's the matter?"

But she looks at Jeffrey, saying, "Zarathustra!"

"What about him?" Jeffrey asks.

"I didn't, like, *leave him any food or water or anything.* My God, he'll *starve!*"

Jeffrey frowns and then returns to his notebook.

"For Christ's sake, don't you hear what I'm *saying?*" Laurel hisses, pulling at his arm.

"I hear," Jeffrey says, lifting his eyes, "but I mean, like what do you expect me to *do?*"

"Is that your cat?" J. Dan asks.

Laurel stares at him for a moment and then nods.

"You should have left him some damn food and water," J. Dan says indignantly, "or else arranged for some damn body to come by and take care of him."

"What in the fuck do you think I've just been *saying?*" Laurel says in a loud, frantic whisper.

Two ranchers at a nearby table raise their faces and stare at her for a minute. Laurel grabs her mouth with her hand and stares at her lap. It is hard to tell whether she is embarrassed or sick at her stomach or both.

"Lower your damn voice," J. Dan says, narrowing his eyes, "or else keep a rein on your damn words."

"God, he'll starve to death," Laurel whispers into her hand, which still clasps her mouth.

"Well, you can't cry over spilt milk," J. Dan declares, starting to pare his fingernails with a pocketknife.

"Christ, I'll have nightmares *forever*, thinking about him!" Laurel says, still holding her mouth. "Like that cat in the tornado! And, I mean, just like our *guppies!*"

"Everybody has something to forget," J. Dan says philosophically, studying his hand as he scrapes blackness from under a heavy thumbnail. "And it is the best thing to try and forget it. Always."

Jeffrey has raised his face from his notebook once again, and stares at J. Dan. "*Nobody* has anything to forget," he says.

"Only if you don't have no memory," J. Dan says, "or sense of decency. Because if you do, sonny boy, you have something to forget."

"Oh, shit," Laurel says, closing her eyes. "Spare me the rancher's Socrates. I mean, I have enough to do to get my shit together without having to listen to wisdom from some raunchy old rancher!"

"Watch your damn language," J. Dan says, returning to his fingernails.

"Well then, watch your stupid moralizing."

Jeffrey seems to contemplate this for a while; then he returns to his notebook when J. Dan says, "Why don't you phone a neighbor and ask her to go over and feed the damn cat?"

Laurel looks thoughtful, but then says, "How would she get in? I mean, I locked the door and everything. At least I *think* I did."

"Don't you have no neighbor you leave a key with?"

"Listen, I don't even *talk* to my neighbors. We like live in different worlds, J. Dan, and you know it."

"That's too bad," J. Dan says.

"Only that back window has a broken latch," Laurel says, grabbing her forehead as if to hold her ideas still. "And that woman next to us . . . couldn't she have her son crawl through it and unlock the back door?"

When Jeffrey doesn't answer her, she shakes his arm, and he looks up and says, "Sure."

"What's their name?" Laurel asks.

"Harris, or something like that," Jeffrey says, scratching his head. He looks outside at the parking lot, then sweeps his gaze vaguely over the other people in the restaurant.

"Harrison," Laurel cries. "And I don't know her husband's first name, but I could ask the information operator for Harrison on Fernway."

"Go on and call," J. Dan says. "And calm your mind down."

"I don't have any money to call. All I have is a dollar bill."

"Just have it put on our bill. Call from the damn motel room."

"Oh, God, I mean, I think I will!" Laurel cries, and hurries away, bumping the table with her hip as she twists out of the booth.

After she leaves, J. Dan raises his head and looks at the counter, saying, "I wonder where our damn breakfast is."

Jeffrey closes his notebook and puts his pen in his shirt pocket. J. Dan yawns, and looks again for his breakfast.

"I don't feel so damn good," he says slowly, rubbing his hand over his tired eyes.

For a while they are silent, and then the waitress brings their breakfasts, and J. Dan hunches over his plate and eats strongly and steadily until it is all gone, all packed away.

28 On her way back to the restaurant, after completing the phone call and making arrangements for the cat, Laurel sees a small, lonely, shapeless figure standing by the driveway entrance to the motel. She stops dramatically and places her palm over her forehead, as if to register great astonishment for all to see.

The figure stares back at her without sign of recognition (although he is a hundred yards away, and she can't see if there actually is any expression on his face). She can, however, see very clearly that the figure is short, fuzzy-headed, dressed in a dirty, too-large British greatcoat, and that it has a guitar slung over its shoulder and a pasteboard sign leaning against its leg.

"Peter Peters!" she cries.

Then she walks up to him, and when she gets close enough, she can see that he is smiling shyly at her. He flashes the peace sign, and Laurel says, "Haven't you gotten to Denver *yet?*"

Peter Peters shakes his head no.

"Well, I mean, *what happened?*"

"Oh, I just been getting rides out of the way," he says. "Two of them. It's all right, I don't mind." For the first time he has spoken a whole sentence to her, and she realizes that he has a slight lisp. It is odd, because the lisp didn't show up at all when he sang in his hoarse, kind of toneless voice.

"Like *where?*" Laurel asks.

"Oh, I don't know," Peter Peters says. "I mean, I don't pay much attention, you know? A lot of people don't know where they're going."

"God, don't I know it!"

"But I been getting a lot of like *rides.*"

"That's good," Laurel says, "because I worried about you. You know, when we got through eating, you were gone."

"I know," Peter Peters says. "I got a ride."

"Did he take you out of the way?"

But Peter Peters doesn't seem to hear the question. He tickles the strings of his guitar absently, and smiles out of his bushel of hair.

"Sing another song, will you?" Laurel asks.

"Right here?"

"Sure. Where else is there?"

Peter Peters seems to like that answer, and he smiles, lifting the guitar as he does so. He has a way of not looking at people, Laurel notices, and not listening very closely. Maybe he is bombed out of his sack.

"Are those like *your own songs?*" she asks.

"I created them," he says shyly. "Composed them, like."

"Nifty," Laurel says, reaching out and touching the shoulder of his greatcoat. It's like he isn't inside the coat at all, because all she can feel is thick, heavy wool. No arm, no shoulder.

Peter Peters starts chording, and then sings:

> Don't worry about no commas or nouns
> Don't worry about no dotted *i*'s
> 'Cause Peters understands those hangin' loose sounds,
> And Peters is the one to open your eyes.
>
> I knew a man once with an up-tight degree
> He got from an up-tight university,
> But this old boy, he don't make it at all,
> And he don't hear nothin' when nobody calls.
>
> Just shake it all loose and say it like it is
> And you gonna find out what's hers and what's his;
> You gonna find out what's right and what's wrong,
> If you listen to my words and listen to my song.
>
> Don't worry about no commas or nouns
> Don't worry about no dotted *i*'s;
> Don't worry about rich ladies in gowns,
> 'Cause they don't know, don't realize.

Peter Peters drops his guitar at his side and smiles into the wind. Laurel reaches out once again, this time shoving a damp and rumpled dollar bill into the pocket of the greatcoat.

"I mean you can buy a cup of coffee with it," she says, embarrassed a little. "Okay? And look: I think your songs are beautiful! No shit; I mean, really *beautiful!*"

114

Smiling, he reaches into his other pocket, withdraws a rumpled sheet with a song dittoed on it in pale purple, and hands it to Laurel. She accepts it, glances at it and tucks it in her CPO pocket. "Okay, it's a sale," she says. "You've sold a copy for a dollar."

Peter Peters smiles in the direction of her head and she turns around and goes to rejoin Jeffrey and J. Dan, saying out loud: "I mean, I can't *believe* it. It's *too much!*"

When she comes back into the restaurant, her breakfast is on the table, and J. Dan says, "It must have been hard getting the call through, it took you so damn long."

"I ran into Peter Peters outside, waiting for a ride," she says. "Of all people!"

She tells them about it while she eats, but Jeffrey and J. Dan, who have finished eating, don't seem to be very impressed by the coincidence, so she stops talking altogether and stares out the window as she chews, only pausing to say, "God, he's a saint!"

After breakfast, they start walking back to the motel room, leaning into the cold wind—J. Dan holding on to his Stetson and Jeffrey hugging his notebook to his side.

"Winter," J. Dan says.

"I'm glad I could get her," Laurel says, repeating everything about the phone call. "And she says she'll have her boy climb through the window after school, and like feed the cat and give him water and everything. I told her she could leave the back door unlocked if she wanted, but she thought that was a bad idea, and said if it wasn't too hard, her boy would crawl through the window once a day until we got back. But I told her just to turn him loose, you know? Zarathustra. I mean, I had to practically like *argue* with her to turn him loose, because he'll get along if he's outside. But anyway, she finally said all right. Fantastic people. Beautiful. I mean, *helpful*, you know?"

They stop at the pickup while J. Dan unlocks the door on his side and begins to rummage around under the seat.

"What's he doing?" Laurel asks, but Jeffrey doesn't answer.

He's squinting into the cold wind, meditating. Finally he says, "You know, I'm really getting it all together."

"What?" Laurel asks.

"Everything. My notes are really beginning to add up, you know? I'm finally getting a philosophy—or like *my* philosophy—of cinema organized . . . or at least it's in the preorganization stage, and it all has to do with this fantastic idea I have of like *e*venting the film, instead of *in*venting it. You know?"

J. Dan crawls back out of the pickup and says, "I've got to go take me a shit."

"Be our guest," Laurel says.

"Don't be such a smart ass," J. Dan says. "What I want to know is, are you two going to stay out here or do you want to come back into the room? Because if you do, I'll lock her up."

"I've got to get my camera and things," Jeffrey says.

"Then I'll lock her up," he says, slamming the door and working the handle up and down.

They follow him inside, but after they get their things together, J. Dan says, "Why don't you two wait outside so I can have me some damn privacy? I won't be long. Here's the keys." He throws them to Jeffrey, who nods and starts for the door.

From the back of the room, J. Dan says, "You can start the damn engine and get her warmed up."

Jeffrey doesn't answer, but closes the door behind Laurel.

"I envy you," Laurel says dreamily, meditatively. "I mean, getting your shit together and everything." The wind blows her hair over one eye and she lifts it away, staring abstractedly into the cold.

"It's like all coming so clear in my mind," Jeffrey says, putting his foot on the front bumper of the pickup, "that it half scares me. And you know something? It's in some strange way all part of this *film*. It's all like coming clear because of *him*. I mean, maybe not *because* of him, but it like has to *do* with him!"

"I haven't written a poem in *weeks*," Laurel says sadly, reciting the words in a faraway voice. "Something's *really* fucking up my head, and I like don't even know where to *turn!*"

"Christ, he's unbelievable. I mean, I can't even begin to tell you."

Laurel glances at him and says, "Well, maybe it'll all come out in the film."

"That's what I'm praying for," Jeffrey says. "You don't have any idea. Like you said: the total film's existence; I'm groping for the damn essence now. You know?"

"I mean, I really envy you, getting it together."

"That's why there have to be shots of everything, clear to the end."

"She certainly won't be so fucking proud and beautiful now, though," Laurel says, putting her hands in the pockets of her jeans and shivering.

"That's not the point," Jeffrey says. "And you know it."

"I don't know anything," Laurel says slowly, meditatively, trying the words out for how they sound.

"It has got to be," Jeffrey says.

"Look at the *dog!*" Laurel cries suddenly, going out behind the pickup to where a little dog is sitting, scratching its ear.

"It's just a puppy," Laurel says, crouching beside it and holding her index finger out. "What kind is it?"

"Looks like it's part beagle," Jeffrey says, coming up and staring down at it with his hands in his pockets. "And part God knows what."

"It's *hungry*," Laurel says, picking it up and cradling it against her CPO jacket.

"Most dogs are," Jeffrey says.

"No, I mean, its *ribs* are showing. Look at them!"

"It does look like it could use a meal," Jeffrey says, poking its side with his knuckles. In response to his touch, the puppy turns and tries to bite his hand.

"Oh, it's *darling!*" Laurel cries.

117

"They're all cute at that age."

"No they're not. Not *this* cute, anyway. Just look at him. He likes me."

"Love at first sight," Jeffrey says, kicking at a piece of gravel with his boot.

"Don't be so fucking cynical," Laurel says.

Jeffrey looks at her and suddenly grins. "Okay, it's cute."

"Cute isn't the word for him: he's *darling!* I wonder if he's a stray or something."

"I wouldn't know."

"I mean, he's not wearing a collar or anything."

"Then he probably is," Jeffrey says.

"Oh, let's take him with us!"

"J. Dan'll have a hemorrhage."

"Well, we won't let him know right away. I can almost get him in my pocket. I mean, he's so *tiny!*"

"Sure, give it a try."

"You know," Laurel says, looking at her reflection in the window of their motel room, "I think I will. The worst he can do is make me give him to somebody in the next town, or something. I mean, he wouldn't make me abandon it out in the open or anything."

"That's hard to predict," Jeffrey says.

"I'll try, anyway."

She takes him to the other side of the pickup, asking Jeffrey to warn her when J. Dan comes out of the motel room. Then she plays with the little dog on the ground. Soon, Jeffrey comes back to watch.

Then, suddenly, J. Dan is there, looking down at the two of them. "What in the hell is that?" he asks.

"It's my new puppy," Laurel says defiantly, casting her hair out of her face as she looks up at J. Dan.

"Well, I'll be damned," J. Dan says.

She snuggles the puppy protectively against her breast and

glares back at him. "He doesn't like *belong* to anybody," Laurel says, "and I'm going to take him with me. He's a poor, sweet, cute, wittle waif."

"He's probably covered with fleas," J. Dan says.

"I don't care. He's all alone and needs me. Jeffrey, please go get a carton of milk from the restaurant. He's hungry. I mean, I can *tell!*"

Jeffrey is standing hunched up against the wind, with his hands in his pockets. He nods, and walks off toward the restaurant.

"It's a damn wonder he has enough money," J. Dan says.

"He's *starving!*" Laurel says, kissing the top of its head, and then holding it in one hand while she unbuttons her CPO jacket so she can snuggle it inside, against the warmth of her breast.

"If it was a damn monkey," J. Dan says wonderingly, "you'd probably by God let it suck on your tit, wouldn't you?"

"I don't see why the fuck not," Laurel says, staring coldly at him. "And I don't see what would be wrong with it. And I'd give it to *him*, too, if he'd take it . . . or if I had milk. Wouldn't I, you sweet little thing?" She says this nuzzling its head again with her face.

When she lifts her head, J. Dan is leaning crookedly against the pickup, rubbing the back of his neck with his hand and staring at her. For an instant they stand this way, without speaking, and then Jeffrey returns with a half-pint carton of milk.

He squats down and opens it up. Laurel kneels down beside him, and places the puppy carefully in front of the carton. They both watch closely as he begins to lap it up.

"God, he's darling!" Laurel whispers passionately.

"He really *is* kind of cute," Jeffrey says. "You know?"

"You and people like you," Laurel says, looking back at J. Dan, "act like you don't even know what your bodies are *for!*"

"What's that all about?" Jeffrey asks, standing up again.

"J. Dan was making fun of me because of the like *maternal* thing," Laurel says, lowering her eyes and caressing the puppy. "I don't know why we even have to listen to people like him."

When it finishes lapping the milk, the puppy trots several steps off and then squats and urinates.

"I love that ethereal look they get when they pee," Laurel says happily, and Jeffrey gives a distant, vague smile.

The puppy starts to trot off with an awkward sideways gait, until Laurel grabs him and lifts him once again to her breast.

"You better button up your damn coat," J. Dan says, "or you'll freeze your puddin'."

"No I won't. I'm not a bit cold. I'm boiling inside."

"He's really cute," Jeffrey says. A Ford camper moves up behind him, and he steps forward to let it pass, without looking at the driver.

"Him's just a wonewy wittle puppy," Laurel says in happy baby talk.

"It's one of them Heinz dogs," J. Dan says. And then, when no one asks him what he means, he explains, "Fifty-seven damn varieties."

"He's his own little purebred, all by himself," Laurel says, with a kissing expression on her lips.

"Well, hell, come on then," J. Dan growls. "You can bring him if you want. A dog *that* damn size we could put in the ashtray and he'd get lost."

"Way to go, J. Dan!" Jeffrey says. "I mean, all *right*, man!"

J. Dan gives him a brief, hard look, and then says, "All right, let's get started. It is getting late."

When they get in the pickup, J. Dan packs a chew of tobacco in his mouth, swelling his right jaw to the size of a tennis ball, and then leans on the starter until the engine catches and rumbles into a smooth, fast idle.

"Faithful Betty Bump," Jeffrey says, smiling and leaning his head tiredly against the window.

"Once more we are off," Laurel says, in her falsetto old-lady voice, and cuddling the puppy to her breast.

J. Dan spits out the window, and once more they are off.

29 NOTE ESSENTIAL PARADOX: NECESSITY TO TRANSFER RE-ALITY TO FILM, WHICH IS ITSELF MEDIUM OF FORGETTING. (OH J. DAN YOU WERE WAITING FOR ME.)

INTRODUCE STOP-MOTION SCENES, LIKE WAY STATION ON JOURNEY. QUEST. STATIONS OF CROSS. (AND DOUBLE CROSS.)

HAVE LIKE JOYCEAN CAPTIONS:

> I'VE TRAVAILED EAST, I'VE TRAVAILED WEST,
> BUT WHERE'ER I GO, HARM IS BREAST.

TITLE: HARM IS WHERE THE HURT IS? (MAYBE, MAYBE NOT.)

J. DAN FALLS INTO THE FILM PRECISELY AS HE FALLS INTO FUTURE. LIKE ALL OF US.

DÉJÀ VU IS WHAT FILM WORKS WITH, LIKE ITS STATEMENT OF MOTIF. (CF. WINDMILLS.)

STOP-MOTION J. DAN (EX. WALKING BACK TO PICKUP) TO FOOT-NOTE HIS SIGNATURE. (FILM A MOVEMENT TO SET OFF, DELINEATE, THE STILL SHOT? YES, HERE'S WHERE I'M GOING.)

ALL THIS UNCLUTTERED LAND IS POWER. IF ONLY CAN BE CLARI-FIED, ARTICULATED. WHY NOT? (THE COMPULSION FOR MOVE-MENT: WANT FILM TO BE AS STABLE, AS INTELLIGENT AS TREATISE, OR NOVEL.) MUST APPROACH POWER AND "FOCUS" OF STILL PHOTO. THE STILL PHOTO AT HEART OF A GREAT FILM.

ALSO CONSIDER BERGMAN POINTS OUT THAT IN 1 HOUR FILM YOU SEE 27 MINUTES DARKNESS (INTERSTICES BETWEEN LIGHTED FRAMES): CHALLENGE IS, ORCHESTRATE, ILLUMINATE THESE INTERSTICES, MAKE THEM WORK IN MIND OF AUDIENCE.

THIS IS METAPHOR, SURE.

KEEP COMING BACK TO J. DAN. FACE FACT: REALLY DON'T UN-DERSTAND WHAT HE'S DOING. FACT HE DOESN'T EITHER IS DODGE:

121

CAN'T ACCEPT THAT. DON'T ACCEPT EXCUSES. SMELL SCENT OF IDEA, FOLLOW.

SOMETHING'S GOING ON. DOWN THERE IN DARKNESS. (IN THOSE 27 MINUTES OF DARKNESS, ANOTHER FILM SHOWING.)

ALL COMES BACK TO HIM, J. DAN, IGNORANT ULYSSES (BUT NO, NOT EXACTLY THAT, EITHER).

GUESS I'VE NEVER SEEN ANYBODY THIS BELIEVING, THIS CONCENTRATED, THIS FOCUSED. J. DAN EVEN SITS IN A CHAIR LIKE HE MEANS IT.

REPEAT: ISN'T THAT HE KNOWS. IT'S WHAT HE DOESN'T EVEN BOTHER TO UNDERSTAND (OR WANT TO UNDERSTAND) THAT'S LUMINOUS. THIS DARK.

IT'S LIKE, J. DAN IS POSSESSED. (NO, NOT THAT EITHER.)

(LAUREL SAYS HE WAS NEVER LIKE THIS BEFORE, SHE CAN'T BUY WHAT HE'S DOING. BUT KEEP TRYING TO TELL HER: HE'S DOING IT.)

FILM STRIVES NOT TO RENDER COHERENT THE HERACLITEAN FLUX, BUT PERPETUATE IT. (MOVING MAP OF UNFOLDING CLOUD.)

BUT NO, NOT THIS EITHER. LIKE ALL ART, FILM EXISTS IN TENSION AGAINST 2 CONTRADICTIONS. WHERE IT IS.

30 They crossed the Colorado border in a few minutes. A half hour later, they saw a sign beside the highway announcing that the elevation was 4,036 feet.

The heater was blowing on their feet and ankles, and J. Dan's batwing window was open, letting cold air trickle across their faces, hands and knees. They rode quietly, half-dazed from the hypnotic flow of dull brown scenery past their eyes. Occasionally, Laurel hugged the puppy and shivered, sending warm vibrations into the shoulders of the men. Jeffrey sighed and put his arm around her. They were uncomfortably crowded, and had been from the start.

"A damn pickup wasn't meant for three people," J. Dan said.

"Well, we're almost there," Jeffrey said.

"Why is he so damn anxious all of a sudden?" J. Dan asked.

"Ask him," Laurel said.

"I *am* asking him. Why are you so damn anxious all of a damn sudden, sonny boy?"

"I told you," Jeffrey said. "I mean, I can understand what you're so intent on. It makes sense to me, and I think it's . . . well, like *beautiful*. You know?"

"I don't see how nothing could be beautiful about it in a thousand damn years," J. Dan said slowly.

"He doesn't *mean* that!" Laurel cried. "And I wish you two had never *seen* each other! What I mean is, I wish you had never made the trip to Wichita in the first place, J. Dan."

"I wish I had never had me a reason to," J. Dan said.

"I think I have to puke," Laurel said.

"Shouldn't we be turning north?" Jeffrey asked. "I mean, off of Route 70?"

"Have you been looking at a map or something?" J. Dan asked suspiciously.

"No, but you said we had to turn north."

"I don't remember saying no such damn thing," J. Dan stated.

"Didn't you say it was in Meeker County, and isn't that to the north?"

"*I* said Meeker County," Laurel said. "When that man who pulled us out of the mud came up and asked us. And you're right, it *is* to the north."

"I never did find out exactly what happened last night," J. Dan commented, shaking his head. "I must have had me a skinful."

"It wasn't much," Laurel said. "We just got somebody to pull us out, and there was this car that came along behind and couldn't pass and was in all this hurry, so Jeffrey just went ahead, hoping he could find a place to turn around, you know, but we had to go farther than we'd thought . . . so anyway, we finally got turned around and came back for you. That's all."

"We carried you up there on the bank because you'd passed out in the mud," Jeffrey said. "We figured you'd be more comfortable up there than in the pickup. And we didn't want to, you know, leave you lying there in the mud."

J. Dan nodded and squinted his eyes. His wad of tobacco bulged like a tumor in his cheek. "It's beginning to snow," he said.

"That must have been part of the nightmare you mentioned," Jeffrey said.

"What was part of *what* nightmare?" J. Dan asked.

"I mean, waking up lying in the field with nobody around, and it was like suddenly dark, you know? And windy and cold."

"Yes," J. Dan nodded. "I guess it was."

"Where do we turn off?" Jeffrey asked again.

J. Dan turned his head to look at him, but Laurel was leaning slightly forward with her eyes closed, as if she were listening. All he could see was her profile and the puppy trying to climb her shoulder.

"In a few miles," J. Dan answered. "We're almost to the turn-off."

But a few miles farther on, there was a jolt in the floorboard, and the pickup slowed down while J. Dan raced the engine several times, without any response.

"There went the damn transmission," J. Dan said in a low voice, as if talking to himself. "The high damn gear, anyway."

"You've got to be kidding," Jeffrey said.

"Something there is," Laurel said in her old-lady voice, "that just doesn't *want* us to get there! I can feel it in my *bones*."

"Shut up a minute, will you?" J. Dan said.

When the pickup had slowed down to thirty, he shifted into super; the gears caught and whined, and the pickup moved up to forty, then forty-five, the transmission whirring.

"Well, she'll get us there," J. Dan said. "Only we won't get there as soon as I'd figured. We won't be doing no damn seventy, *that's* for sure."

"Poor Betty Bump," Laurel said, nuzzling the dog. "She's having a breakdown!"

She turned to Jeffrey, hoping to evoke some response from him, but he had obviously seen nothing humorous in what she said, and ignored her, looking out his side window, frowning slightly.

A sign announcing the north turnoff glided toward them, and Jeffrey said, "At last."

A half hour after they had made the turn, they came to a small town, and J. Dan pulled into a filling station, saying, "I can use me some gas. Not only that, I want to get me a damn 7-Up for my stomach."

Jeffrey got out his notebook. Laurel closed her eyes and leaned her head back against the seat, feeling the puppy squirm in her lap. She said she like *felt sick at her stomach again.*

31 At the town's third and last traffic light, J. Dan turns swiftly right, without announcing his intention to the other two, and they lean away from the turn and press against his shoulders.

"*Now* what are you up to?" Laurel says, wiping her hair out of her eyes, and leaving her mouth slightly open.

"I have got to make me one more stop," J. Dan says.

He coasts along the street, the transmission whirring, and stops before a parking place. He twists in his seat and looks back as he eases the pickup neatly into it, and then he turns back and switches off the ignition.

"What are you doing?" Laurel asks.

"I am going to get me a couple pints of Old Charter," J. Dan says. "A hair of the damn dog. Do you two want anything?"

"No," Laurel says.

"Nothing," Jeffrey says, looking out the window.

J. Dan nods, climbs out of the pickup, and then spits before closing the door.

Jeffrey returns to his notebook, and Laurel starts humming "There's a New Man and Woman Born This Day."

"What's taking him so long," Jeffrey says after a while. She is suddenly aware that he has closed his notebook and is sitting there waiting . . . a little tense and maybe like *suspicious*, even.

"I don't know," she says.

A few minutes later, she hears the sound of Jeffrey's camera, and looks up to see J. Dan approaching the pickup. He is carrying two bottles in a sack. When he is about twenty feet away, he sees Jeffrey and pauses to spit ostentatiously on the curb, still looking at him. Then he briefly rubs one big brown hand over his eyes and continues toward them, moving slowly, with exaggerated articulation, as if programmed by the slow-motion phasing of the camera.

When he comes up to the pickup, he jerks the door open on Jeffrey's side and says, "Okay, sonny boy, you have just reached the end of the damn line."

"What are you talking about?" Jeffrey asks.

"When I said a pickup wasn't meant for three people," J. Dan says, "I meant every damn word. You have had it, sonny boy, so get your ass out of there right this minute." He fumbles in his pocket and finally manages to withdraw a ticket, which he vibrates six inches in front of Jeffrey's face.

"Look," Jeffrey says, "I'm *with* you in this thing. We're almost there."

"You got it wrong," J. Dan says. "This here is a bus ticket. I asked them back there at the filling station if they was a damn bus that stopped here, going east, and they told me yes, by God, they have one going east at eleven-twenty, which is what you are going to get your smart ass on. I have taken every bit of shit I am ever in my whole life going to take from you, and if you don't climb out of there right now, I am going to bust you all over this damn sidewalk."

"Look," Jeffrey says, leaning back into Laurel, away from J. Dan.

"*You* look. I remember what you said last night about taking some damn movie pictures of Laurel's mother, and there is no way that I am going to put up with a fucking little pervert like you that would even *think* of doing such a thing! Do you understand, sonny boy? Now haul your skinny little ass out of there right now, or so help me, I will soon be stepping in your damn brains!"

"J. Dan, for Christ's sake, stop!" Laurel cries. But it is as if the cry itself triggers the assault, for J. Dan in one motion drops the bus ticket and sack of bottles and grabs Jeffrey's arm with his left hand, and then pulls him violently forward precisely as he slams his right fist in his face. Once, twice, three times, while Jeffrey's arms grope thickly and vaguely to ward off the blows.

Laurel screams and lunges across to swing her fist at J. Dan's face. Her first blow misses, but then she hits his neck with one blow, still screaming into his face, as he raises his eyes and stares somberly at her, like a man standing calm and knee-deep in a raging torrent. She hits him again, and this time makes his nose bleed a little.

Then they are both breathing at each other, staring for an instant into each other's eyes, while Jeffrey is on his hands and knees, lurching against J. Dan's leg, blood pouring from his nose and mouth onto the sidewalk.

"What in the hell is going on here?"

J. Dan and Laurel both turn to see a young policeman, wearing a gun belt and a Stetson, standing there jumpy and white-faced, looking from one of them to the other.

Jeffrey turns over on the sidewalk and sits there staring out of dull eyes, his mouth and nose smeared with bright blood, which drops slowly on his dirty T-shirt.

"This is a private matter," J. Dan says formally, taking a red bandanna and wiping his own nose.

"Well, hell, we'll just have to *see* about that!" the officer says, pulling out his notebook.

Jeffrey slowly stands up; and Laurel, who is now outside the pickup, swings at J. Dan's face, hitting the side of his head.

"Oh, you son of a bitch!" she cries.

There is a crowd of people standing around them now, and the police officer—who is very young, fresh-cheeked, with pale, angry eyes—says, "That's enough of that, now. I want your names and addresses, damn it. And no more fighting."

"My name is J. Dan Swope," J. Dan says.

"Are you drunk?" the officer asks.

Suddenly they are all aware that they are standing in the thick strong reek of bourbon. J. Dan leans over and picks up the sack, now clanking from one of the pint bottles, which is broken. The other one is all right.

"I just broke a damn bottle," J. Dan says. "But I haven't had me a single damn drink today."

"Is he drunk?" the officer asks Laurel.

"No, he's not drunk."

Jeffrey is now leaning against the fender of the pickup, blotting blood from his face with a wad of Kleenexes a woman has given him.

"He's a damn hitchhiker," J. Dan says, sniffing, "and I just told him he wasn't welcome no longer, and to haul ass. He wouldn't go, so I busted him. Here's his damn ticket I just bought him to go back to Wichita, where he belongs. Where he shouldn't ever have left in the first place."

"Now wait just a minute," the cop says. "Wait just a minute. Are there any witnesses?"

"Look, I'm all right," Jeffrey says. "I won't press any charges. And I'm not a hitchhiker. This is my girl friend, and he's her stepfather. Her mother is dying of cancer, and she's trying to get back to see her. Okay? I mean, I'm the only one who's suffered any like *damage,* and I won't press charges if you let us get on our way."

"Officer," J. Dan says, "this fucking creep wants to take *pictures.* I mean, he's got something *wrong* with him. He's been a pain in the ass ever since we left *Wichita!*"

"Hold on, hold on," the cop says, shoving his Stetson back behind his ears. A small frown crimps the insides of his eyebrows, and he takes two or three audible breaths before continuing.

"First of all," he says, "watch your obscene language out here on the street." He turns to Laurel and Jeffrey and says, "That goes for all of you. Now, second, I don't know what you're talking about when you say he wants to take pictures. Incidentally, are there any witnesses?"

He turns around to the crowd, but nobody volunteers anything, until an old man coughs and says, "All I seen was this here cowboy knock the young one on his ass. Gave him a *real* good bust, I'd call it!"

"That's what more of them need," another old man's voice growls, and several people laugh.

"Hell, it wasn't nothing but a fight!" a fat man with glasses says. "Andy, you ain't going to make that much fuss over a damn *fistfight,* are you?"

The cop shakes his head and sighs. "I don't like to see all that red blood over our sidewalks is all. Where you from, Mr. Swope?"

"Meeker County," J. Dan says.

"Well, hell," the cop says, putting his notebook back in his hip pocket. Then he turns to Jeffrey and says, "You say you don't want to press charges?"

"No," Jeffrey says. "Providing I don't have to go back. I mean, I belong with Laurel. Her." He points to Laurel's left breast. The cop looks at the breast and nods. Then he looks up at Laurel and says, "Okay with you?"

"All right," she says, not looking at him or anybody else.

"You're not hurt, are you?" he asks, turning back to Jeffrey.

"No, I'm all right. I think. I mean, my lip's cut and everything, but I guess I'm okay."

The cop leans over closer and says, "You're going to have a shiner, too. He busted you on your nose and eye *both!*"

"I warned him," J. Dan says. "A *hundred* damn times."

"Well, if you're going to have a feud, take it outside the corporation limits," the cop says, satisfied that he has handled the situation well. He walks away, and the crowd begins to scatter.

"That was a damn beauty," one of the old men who had spoken up says to J. Dan. J. Dan looks at him for an instant, and then nods. The man shakes his head admiringly and walks away.

"All right," J. Dan says to Jeffrey. "You win this round, too, it looks like. Get back in."

"Aren't you going to turn the bus ticket in?" Laurel asks, picking the puppy up off the floorboard as she climbs back into the pickup.

"No, I can do that any time. The thing to do now is just plain damn *get* there before it's too *late!*"

"That's right," Jeffrey says. J. Dan looks at him sharply, and then concentrates on the rear-vision mirror before turning out into traffic.

Laurel says, "Do you know something? You two have been so busy hating each other and fighting each other that you haven't even bothered to consider *me!* And I would think this concerns *me* more than anyone else. I mean, it's bad enough that you have to force me to go see her, but if you do, you might at least *consider* me once in a while. God, I mean, it's no *wonder* my head's so fucked up! I can't even make *notes* for my poetry, let alone *write* poetry!"

"Who are you talking to?" Jeffrey says.

"I'm talking to *both* of you!" she cries, sounding almost hysterical.

"Jesus, she's *crazy!*" Jeffrey whispers, dropping his head heavily against the window.

"And who wouldn't be, going through what *I've* had to go through ever since you talked me into this shitty trip!"

Jeffrey says, "J. Dan, you win, man. I mean, don't ever doubt it: you win."

"I feel like I'm about ready to barf," Laurel cries, clasping the squirming puppy to her stomach.

"We're almost there," J. Dan says. "Everybody, just hang on. Because we're almost there."

32 THERE'S NOT ONLY GENERALLY AND OBVIOUSLY (CLICHÉ) THIS FILM LANGUAGE, THIS FILM DICTION, GRAMMAR, PUNCTUATION, AND ESP. SYNTAX. BUT MORE IMPORT. A FILM VOICE. LIKE, VOICE IMPLICIT IN J. DAN'S MANIA.

FORGET PAST. (HIS MADNESS.) I MEAN, IT HAS POISONED ENOUGH. ALWAYS FORGET. AGAIN: FILM AS MEDIUM OF FORGETTING. ERGO, PARADOX OF NECESSITY TO TRANSCRIBE ALL THIS JOURNEY ON FILM, EVERYTHING, IN ORDER TO RENDER IT FORGETTABLE. FILM A DRAIN THAT TIME FLOWS DOWN.

WHICH SAYS, FILM WRITES NAMES ON WATER (REAL NAMES, NOT PUBLIC ONES). FILM HAS NOTHING INSIDE. ART OF SURFACES, WHERE J. DAN DOESN'T FIGURE. OR DOESN'T FIGURE HE FIGURES. PLATO'S CAVE AGAIN. WHY NOT? PLATO GAVE ONLY HALF TRUTH. SAW HIS OWN SHADOWS. FILM STIMULATES PERSONAL REACTION. (REACTION VS. THOUGHT.)

WHAT IS NOTATION ASKED FOR. ASK AGAIN AND AGAIN. AND NEVER REPEAT NOTATIONS WITHIN CEREMONY OF REPETITION AT HEART OF FILM SENSE. LIKE, "VARIATIONS ON COMPULSIVE THEME."

BERGMAN SAYS FILM IS DECEIT. REPEAT. REPEAT. DECEIT. EXPLOITS HUMAN WEAKNESS. BUT NEED THIS LIKE FLUORIDE IN WATER, LIKE PASTURIZATION OF MILK.

ON OTHER HAND, CONTRADICT. WANT TO MAKE THIS LAPIDARY

131

ART, CONCERNED WITH BEAUTIFUL AND ELUSIVE JEWEL OF LIGHT. (YEATS'S SHAPING OF AGATE.) IN MAKING DESIGN TO DISCOVER TRUTH. MAKE IT HARD, STABLE, <u>STILL</u>.

SPEAKING OF Y., FILM REVEALS THOUGHTS IN WHOLE BODY. THAT'S ALL IT <u>CAN</u> REVEAL.

ERGO COME BACK TO THOSE 27 MINS. DARK IN EVERY HOUR OF FLICKS.

MAYBE ENLARGE THESE INTERVALS—SLOW DOWN SEQUENCE FRAMES IN PROJECTOR AND DELIBERATELY FLICK AGAIN, GIVING DARK A COUNTERPOINT. (THE DARK INTERVALS J. DAN'S. BROOD ON THIS: SOMETHING HERE.) THE FLICKS WHERE THE 27 MINS. EXPAND AND ARE <u>SEEN</u>. (TRUTH A DEEPER SHADOW: THIS MAKES REALITY COHERENT.)

WANTED TO FILM HER MOTHER'S DEATH AS TELEOLOGICAL SIGNATURE (LIKE FRENCH HORN AND CONTRABASSOON DRONING IN BACKGROUND AGAINST DARK BLOWING CURTAINS, SLOW-MOTION, AND LAP-DISSOLVING INTO HEAD AND FACE OF DYING WOMAN. DARK GIVING BIRTH TO HER, SHE'S LIKE BEING BORN TO DEATH).

BUT CHRIST DON'T KNOW NOW. MAYBE THAT IS PART OF DARKNESS I NEED IN THIS. SOME THINGS ONLY SHOW IN DARK.

ISN'T THIS WHAT I'VE BEEN SAYING, TRYING TO SAY?

LIKE J. DAN WILL NOT TALK ABOUT PAST, SPECIFICS. BUT REMEMBERS BECAUSE THAT'S WHY HE'S DRAGGED US ALL THIS WAY. HE SAID YOU <u>HAVE</u> TO FORGET, WHICH IS STATEMENT OF MEMORY.

CONCEPTION CHANGING.

MAYBE TOO MUCH DAMNED INTERFERENCE.

LIKE, LET THINGS HAPPEN. WATCH. KEEP SILENT. REMEMBER. WHY NOT? EVENT THE FILM. THIS IS REALLY WHERE I'M AT. MUSTN'T FORGET.

J. DAN WALKING THROUGH STORM OF CONCEPTIONS, SHEDDING THEM LIKE RAIN. RENDER THIS IN SCENE? SUPERIMPOSE RAIN LIKE SOUND.

J. DAN RUMINATING.

LIKE, WHAT GOES ON IN HEAD. BACKGROUND. GESTALT. (ANY-

ONE'S HEAD.) SOMETHING GETTING TOGETHER HERE, FIGURE. CON-
CEPTION CHANGING. THAT IS, MAYBE HAVE ENOUGH FILM AL-
READY. TAKE THAT 27 MINS. AND EXPAND TO HOUR AND HALF,
PHASING FRAMES TO GLOW INTO LIGHT SLOWLY, THEN GLIMMER
OUT. MAYBE TAKE STANDARD SPEED SHOTS OF THIS AS TRANSLATED
BY PROJECTOR ON SCREEN.

ENOUGH EXIST. TO CONTAIN THE BURGEONING ESS.

THIS TELEOLOGICAL PATTERN CONTRA LITERAL SEQUENCE OF
DYING WOMAN.

BECAUSE J. DAN WON'T SHOW IN DYING WOMAN. HAVE TO DE-
CIDE SOON. ALMOST THERE. DON'T KNOW. NOW FILM'S EVENT-
ING BY ITSELF. I'M TRULY ALONG FOR THE RIDE.

33 North of town, the road is still narrower, twisting
through vast and high rolling plains, cold and wind-rubbed, des-
olate and stark behind an occasional shed or ranch house.

After twenty minutes, Laurel is weeping in her hands, the two
men sitting beside her ride in stony indifference to the blub-
bery noises she makes.

Then there are a few minutes of silence, after which she leans
over to Jeffrey and says, "Listen, I don't want to go any farther;
I'm sick at my stomach. I can't stand the thought of it. I don't
want to go back. Help me."

But Jeffrey merely shakes his head no, and refuses to look at
her.

J. Dan opens his window and spits, a grave and dignified expression on his face. His skin looks a little pale and dirty. His
face is still lopsided from an enormous plug of tobacco. He
doesn't feel good either.

The snow continues to fall in flurries, but shortly before they
arrive, a great cloud to the south separates, filling the cold and

vacant land with sunlight. For the first time since J. Dan had hit him, Jeffrey lifts his camera and shoots through the window.

"I thought the reflection on the glass interfered," Laurel says.

"It does," Jeffrey says, nodding. "But that's all right. I mean, that's part of it too. Don't let it bother you: the film is packed inside all this footage like the meat of a nut inside the shell. What we have to do, after we take all those thousands of feet of footage, is find it. I mean. It's there waiting. Like all the time: *imprisoned!*"

Laurel looks thoughtful, and then nods, obscurely comforted by his conviction, his courage, his vision, his stubbornness, his eventual relevance.

They pass a used-car lot, a stained-wood tavern, and a pink cement-block Laundromat on one side of the road; a red brick motel and a stained-wood antique shop on the other. Then there is a wide expanse of autumn-bleached lawn to the left, beyond which lies a low, pale, brick building, flanked by asphalt parking areas. Above a tiny cement island in one of these, an American flag blows vividly toward the east, whipping rhythmically in their direction as they begin to circle toward the building.

"This is it," J. Dan says.

Laurel lifts her pale face and stares.

J. Dan eases the pickup against one of the concrete barriers placed like chevrons at the edge of the asphalt. He turns off the ignition. Then, not even seeming to look, he reaches across Laurel's lap with a sudden gesture and grabs Jeffrey's camera out of his hands.

In almost the same movement, he swings open the door on his side and slams the camera down on the asphalt. When he steps out of the pickup, he lifts his right boot and methodically, slowly stamps it until it is completely mashed and broken.

When he comes to the front of the pickup, Jeffrey and Laurel are looking at him distantly.

Jeffrey says, "All right, now you've done it. But that doesn't change anything." His voice is mild, regretful.

"Come on," J. Dan says. "She is waiting for us."

He escorts them up the front walk and through the heavy, tinted-glass doors, into a blue-carpeted waiting room. A reception desk at one end is vacant, but as J. Dan approaches it, a tall, well-groomed woman comes out into the waiting room and asks him if she can help.

"Yes," J. Dan says, in a formal voice, "we have come to see Mrs. Burch. Florence Burch. This here's her daughter, who has come to see her."

"Oh, yes," the woman says, recognizing J. Dan. "Just take a seat, Mr. Swope, and I'll see if it's all right."

She leaves the room again, and J. Dan looks around and notices that no one else is waiting. "Visiting hours aren't until two-thirty," he explains, but neither Jeffrey nor Laurel hears him.

Laurel goes over to the long front window and looks out. Jeffrey sits down and leafs blindly through a magazine.

When the woman returns, she nods, and then leads all of them down a long hall, and then halfway down another, where she enters a room briefly and then comes back out.

"These aren't visiting hours," she explains, "but I remember you, Mr. Swope, and it will be all right if you don't stay too long right now. You can stay longer if you come back later this afternoon."

"We'll be back," J. Dan says.

"Just go right in," the woman says.

J. Dan opens the door, steps inside the tiny room and says, "Well, Florence, they are here."

The dying woman is lying pale and emaciated on her back. Her skin is soft and white, and her once-beautiful eyes are grotesquely ringed with deep, dark, morbid shadows. Her neck is scrawny and taut. Her hair is in curlers.

For an instant, Laurel stares at her, and then she moans and rushes to the bed, where she drops to her knees and buries her face in the mattress.

"Oh, baby!" her mother croaks, and reaches out blindly, trying to touch her head. Finally she finds it, and caresses it weakly.

Laurel is now weeping hysterically and clutching her mother's hand with both of hers, and Florence is saying, "Baby, baby, why don't you wash your hair?" Her voice is weak, far away. J. Dan is looking dazed. Jeffrey is watching everything. The room is hot and smells of old hay, of wasted flesh, of chewing tobacco, of death.

"It'll be all right, baby," Florence says. Her lips hardly move; her entire face is numb.

Eventually, Laurel's crying subsides, and she is now resting the side of her head on the mattress, facing away from her mother and blinking out at nothing. Now and then she sniffs.

"Aren't you going to kiss me, J. Dan?" Florence says weakly.

"Sure," J. Dan says, going over and kissing her on the forehead, then on the mouth.

"Oh, it was good of you to come, baby," Florence says passionately, once more touching her daughter's hair. "It all seems so unreal, now. So pointless and sad. Like we don't ever have to make one another unhappy. Not *ever!*"

"This here's her boy friend," J. Dan says, pointing to Jeffrey with his thumb.

Florence speaks inaudibly and tries to smile, but no one understands what she's said. "What's that?" J. Dan asks.

"I said I thought that's who it was," Florence says.

Her voice is indistinct and far away. She speaks as if her upper lip were paralyzed. And to keep her eyes open, she has to raise her eyebrows, as if her lids are numb.

"It was good of you, J. Dan," she says.

"It wasn't no more than what was right," J. Dan says, righteously.

"Yes it was, to bring my baby back."

Jeffrey is sitting down in the room's only chair, squeezed in beside a small white enamel table.

A bell rings remotely in the hall, and J. Dan says, "I am going to have to go and take me a shit. I'll be back in a few minutes."

He leaves the room and goes down the hall until he comes to the toilet, where he goes in, removes his Stetson and washes his face in hot water. Then he smoothes his hair down with both hands, stares at his reflection in the mirror an instant, and goes into the second booth and drops his pants.

34 "Take care of him until I get well," Florence said.

Laurel raised her head and stared at her mother. "What was that?" she asked.

"Cook for him and see that his laundry gets done," Florence said. "Please. I'll make it up to you somehow."

Laurel swallowed and turned a stricken look to Jeffrey, who lowered his eyes.

"This medicine," Florence said, pausing to catch her breath, "makes me so groggy I can't hardly tell whether I'm asleep or awake. It's all like a muddy sort of dream, baby."

The nurse came in and said, "I'm sorry, but I think you'd better go, now. Where's the other one?"

"He went to the bathroom," Laurel said. She was standing by the window, her face darkened by the light from the Venetian blinds. Jeffrey still sat in the chair, hunched forward with his hands clasped between his knees, staring at the corner of the bed.

"I'll tell him when he comes back," the nurse said. "You two can wait out in front, in the waiting room. Okay?"

"He should be back now," Laurel said.

"Well, you can wait out there. It's time for medication. You can come back during visiting hours. Can't they?"

She addressed this to Florence, who nodded with an otherworldly expression on her face, like someone in the midst of a yawn that won't stop.

"Go on, now," the nurse said.

Laurel squeezed her mother's hand, and then kissed her forehead.

Jeffrey said good-by and went out into the hallway.

When Laurel joined him, her face was pale and taut. "God, she doesn't even *know!*" she whispered.

Jeffrey nodded, and then put his arm around her and led her toward the waiting room in front.

The nurse left the room, and in a few minutes, J. Dan came back with a fresh chew of tobacco packed in his cheek.

Florence didn't recognize him right away, but when she did, she said, "The nurse sent them out. They're waiting out in front."

"Well, we'll be back this afternoon," J. Dan said.

Florence turned her head a little and looked at him. "What's wrong with his face?" she said. "It looks like he's been hurt."

"I had to smack his damn face for him," J. Dan said.

"I thought you were through with doing crazy things like that, J. Dan. Were you drunk?"

"No. He had this idea of taking pictures of you, and . . . well, taking pictures of all of us. It's too much to go into, now."

"Taking pictures?"

"Well, there was more than that. But that was part of it."

"Why would you hit him for wanting to do that?"

"Look, why don't you just forget it," J. Dan said, patting her shoulder. "That's all water over the dam so far as I'm concerned."

"You know," Florence said, "we never did have our picture taken together. You and Laurel and me. And yet, you're the only real family I have, now. Or ever will have, I guess."

"Don't talk that way," J. Dan said. His eyes glistened a little as he shifted his tobacco to the other cheek.

"It would be nice, wouldn't it?" Florence said, after a pause.

"What would?"

"Oh, just to have a picture of the three of us. Just us three together."

J. Dan rubbed his eyes with his hand for a moment. "I guess so, if you really want one," he said.

"There's that camera at home in the bedroom closet," Florence said.

The nurse came back into the room and told J. Dan he would have to leave.

"We'll be back this afternoon," J. Dan said. "Don't worry none about *that!*"

"I know," Florence said. "And I'll have my hair down by then."

The nurse gave J. Dan a hard look, so he kissed Florence and left the room.

When he escorted Laurel and Jeffrey out the front door, he said, "I am going to take you down to a little store in town and buy you both some decent damn clothes. Do you both understand?"

"Whatever you want," Laurel said. "I'm through arguing. I mean, I feel like I'm stoned or something, you know?"

Jeffrey nodded, but he wasn't looking at anything.

"God, I didn't realize it would affect me this way," Laurel continued as they approached the pickup. She lifted her hair out of her eyes with a tired hand, and stared soberly at the asphalt of the parking lot as she walked.

"She must have been like really beautiful," Jeffrey said.

"Oh, God, she *was!*" Laurel said. "The most beautiful woman who ever lived!"

They came to the pickup and J. Dan unlocked the door on their side. When Laurel climbed up into her seat, she saw that the dog had peed on it, right in the middle, in *her* place.

"He doesn't know any better," Laurel said, wiping the pee up with a Kleenex, and taking the puppy in her lap.

"She must have looked a lot like you," Jeffrey said in a low voice, after he had climbed up beside her.

"More beautiful by any standard," Laurel said. "She used to sing to me at night, before I'd go to sleep. You know, nursery-rhyme songs and things." Her voice broke, and she sniffed.

J. Dan climbed in behind the steering wheel, and Jeffrey said, "I know."

When J. Dan started the pickup, Laurel said, "I'm glad your fucking camera was broken."

The pickup started backing up, with J. Dan twisted around to see, and Jeffrey said, "I mean, I wouldn't have taken pictures *then,* for God's sake! What I had in mind was . . . never mind, forget it."

"You know, people really do *die!*" Laurel muttered, looking down at the puppy she was holding in her lap.

"I've heard tell they do," Jeffrey said vaguely. "Like my father. He told me that by doing it. Show, don't tell."

"Oh, God," Laurel whispered, "I can't stand it!"

"There is nothing else to do," Jeffrey said.

"That's right," J. Dan said, and Laurel turned to gaze at him steadily for a full minute, as he guided the pickup through the noon traffic of their little town.

When J. Dan managed to find a parking place for the pickup, the sun had come out again, and the snow flurries had stopped. The temperature, however, had dropped still further. The Meeker County National Bank showed 11:23 on one side of its rotating sign, and 24° on the other.

J. Dan took them to Preston's Clothing Store and introduced them to the owner, Reed Preston himself, a bald, skull-faced man wearing gold-rimmed glasses and a Paisley vest.

"Reed," J. Dan said, "I want you to fix these two up with complete everything and put it on my personal damn bill. Okay?"

"It'll be a pleasure, J. Dan," the man said, trying not to look at Laurel and Jeffrey.

J. Dan turned back to them and said, "And when you're through, come over across the street and up a ways"—he paused and pointed through the front display window—"to the Crazy Horse Bar and Grill and we'll have us some lunch. Now don't forget, and no damn tricks, because I will be, by God, there waiting!"

"We won't," Laurel said. "Honest to God, you don't have anything to worry about."

"We've got something you young folks might like," Reed Preston said. "They're the latest thing: pre-faded jeans."

J. Dan looked at him, and Preston said, "Smartest idea in years. None of these young people like new-looking clothes, so these people came out with jeans, shirts, the whole thing, *pre-faded.*"

J. Dan shook his head wonderingly.

"You know, it's kind of like what they call 'distressing' in antiques. Same idea."

"Well," J. Dan said, "they will probably think it's just fine. And it don't make any damn difference to me. Just so they're new and clean."

"Oh, they're new and clean, all right," Preston said, throwing some plaid-lined, pre-faded jeans over the counter for Laurel and Jeffrey to look at.

J. Dan nodded and left the store. Outside, the cold sunny air revived him a little, and he felt better.

But he didn't go directly to the Crazy Horse Bar and Grill. Instead, he got back in the pickup, and drove out of town toward his ranch house, eight miles away, where Florence had said there was a camera on the bedroom-closet shelf.

Of course he remembered seeing the thing around there somewhere, but he couldn't remember whether he had seen it on the shelf of the closet or not.

Still, it had to be around there. And he would surely have

time to find it and get back to the Crazy Horse Bar and Grill before Laurel and Jeffrey had finished shopping.

35 Smoke begins to rise from the street and curl lazily out of windows, long, dirty-gray tatters of air that float toward the smudged sun as if coiling upward in response to another, a hypothetical, gravity.

J. Dan walks along a fence row, checking the strands of wire, the staples, the posts. There is a thick odor of cattle manure in the air, along with the heaviness of winter. Something iron in the cold breaks with each step he takes forward, and his progress is itself iconoclastic and hard. His eyes are creased, his mouth is set, his expression is grim.

A hundred miles away, Florence's headstone is being carved, the letters incused in the stone slowly coming into shape, like frames of a time-phase photograph waxing, waning, and dropping off into dark.

J. Dan is running in the high grass, slow-motion, his worn leather boots kicking up dust each time they hit and dig into the alkaline soil. J. Dan is crying out, his voice inaudible. A bassoon grovels in the foundation earth of sound, squirting little green shoots of guitar melody into the darkening air.

A fire is burning like an inverted skirt up a telephone pole. Florence lifts her eyebrows, not moving the eyelids themselves, for she is blinded with pain and obfuscation.

The telephone pole is isolated in an infinite terrain. There is nothing around it. After it has burned black and lost all its filigrees of flame, it starts tiredly to turn at the top, like an abstract windmill, and then drops its festoons of wire and becomes yet something else, in a slow, vague metamorphosis of fact.

The frames flip over, introduced irrelevantly into a cast-iron flip-card viewer in a penny arcade. Suddenly, in the midst of

"Maisie Takes Off Her Clothes," there is a sequence of slowly rotating burned-out telephone poles in a vacant land.

Elsewhere, J. Dan drinks and sees his Stetson turning slowly away, rolling eccentrically like a faded, light, and crooked ghost of a ball into the blighted flatnesses of the dream, the sleep, the land.

Turning away from the monotonous, persistent lens, he reaches up into the secrecies of the closet, and withdraws the camera she said was there.

At which vision, she raises her eyebrows (still unable to lift the heavy, hardened lids) and smiles, saying, "Yes, yes, thank you, J. Dan, and won't you kiss me, my darling, my true, my only love? My handsome prince? My daddy, my darling, my mad dumb man?"

Now, the goat-faced young man with the camera is seen, three-quarter back view, and turns around to look at this other lens, an expression of confusion seeping upward in his face until he understands and rubs his hand across his chin, rubbing away the beard as if it were clots of hair, and then thinking, holding his hand up again, but this time to shield his image from the blinding sensitivity to brainless light, and turning away, leaning over to pick up a battered Stetson and holding it like a camera, but eventually putting it on his head, to rest his seeing eyes in the shade it affords, for there is now a hard vector of light intersecting the quadrilateral cage of the shot.

Eisenstein rises to a sitting position and nods.

Bergman closes his book and says something brilliantly equivocal.

The afterthought of Griffith stands superbly aristocratic and strong, intellectual and cool, regarding the further metamorphosis of his art.

Florence caresses the head of her baby and says, "Honey, wash your damn *hair!*"

J. Dan snores, asleep in the chair where he sat down, dreaming he is dreamed, dreamed he is dreaming. His two greyhounds have been let inside, and they are asleep at his feet. The dogs look good—Bill Banks has taken good care of them.

The camera moves, whirs, hiccups, lists, records, regurgitates, forgets. No thought intervenes between it and what it records. Jeffrey studies the mathematics of effects, and then makes notations on a dying face.

J. Dan groans and twists his head.

He awakens and goes into the tiny bathroom and shaves, feeling the cold light from outside on his bare shoulder, and all that land beyond, where his cattle are grazing. And beyond that, vastly out of sight, mountains.

Oh, yes.

The film is running, even after Jeffrey has forgotten.

And it was running before he came, before his participation. And beyond his understanding.

There is a stubborn smell of cattle, the despair of flesh, the forgetting of manure ("The past is *shit*," Laurel's voice says), in the flow of cold air through the curtains.

J. Dan is lonely and turns on the television set in the front room. It was turned on before so that he would hear a voice as he shaved.

Yes, it is all being recorded.

J. Dan has fallen asleep, but he is awake within ten minutes, knowing that indeed, in truth, all is well, for he has not slept long.

Then he puts on his coat and goes back out to the battered pickup, which has been grazing idly during his absence.

And starts driving in second gear down the cold dirt road toward town, where they are waiting, and she is dying.

He has completed and fulfilled his obligation, and even underneath all the despair and fatigue, there is a peace that others could seldom understand.

The dirt road rolls heavily, slowly, firmly, inevitably under the wheels, and he is once more in the outskirts of town, headed toward the Crazy Horse Bar and Grill.

144

Beside a little azure cement-block house near the edge of town, there is a horse grazing. The horse's eye, like a moving camera, catches the fleeting image of his pickup as it rolls heavily and carelessly past.

There is no parking place, and J. Dan stubbornly circles the block three times, determined not to walk far . . . as if he might have to run to the pickup within seconds and get started on some other equally inscrutable journey.

The sign on the Meeker County National Bank says 12:27 and, on the other side, 23°.

J. Dan wipes his strong hand over his eyes and enters the Crazy Horse Bar and Grill, loaded for bear.

36 "I guess we did right after all," Laurel says. "I mean, in spite of everything I feel good seeing her. You know? I'm sorry, but I think he was right. I have to be like *honest to my deepest feelings* and say it's true. You know?"

"Don't apologize," Jeffrey says, "unless you're sure of what you're doing. No, I take that back: don't apologize for any reason. J. Dan wasn't *all* right."

"I mean, shit, who *is?*"

"I don't mean that, either." Jeffrey is alert, a little wary. He is aware that something of slightly greater importance is happening between Laurel and himself, and he isn't sure what.

"Look," she says, "all I'm saying is *both* of you were right. I mean, you were as up tight as he was at the end."

"Forget it," Jeffrey says. "I want to think. I don't want to talk. All right?"

As if answering him, Laurel steps off the curb by mistake, and turns her ankle. She hisses with pain, and then limps on one foot until Jeffrey collects her in his arms, as if she were really heading for him.

"You okay?" Jeffrey asks.

Laurel limps away from him and says, "I thought I'd never live to hear you ask."

"I mean your ankle or something," Jeffrey says, shrugging his shoulders and smiling in exasperation directly into the sunlight.

"You and J. Dan have this thing," Laurel says. "I don't even know what it *is!*"

"It's over now," Jeffrey says. "In a way, anyway. Or *almost* over."

"But what *is* it? I mean, like what *was* it?"

"Too long and difficult to say," Jeffrey says, frowning up into the crystal air at the traffic light. Laurel follows his look, and sure enough, they are waiting to cross one of the few main streets in town. Waiting for them on the other side is the Crazy Horse Bar and Grill.

"That's where he's waiting," Laurel says, pointing with her knee.

"Your ankle all right?" Jeffrey asks again.

"Yes, I'll live," Laurel says. "If you can call existence in this place living."

"Forget it," Jeffrey says.

"Still, as I said, I'm glad he got his way. J. Dan. I mean, in spite of everything, he was right. You know?"

"I only wish you'd like shut up," Jeffrey says.

The light changes and they cross the street, following the trail of their steaming breaths that the cold breeze blows before them.

Their dumpy shadows are strong and intense, darting step by step with them under their bodies.

"The thing that gets me," Laurel says, as they reach the other curb, "is that she doesn't even *know*. I mean, it's like she's been translated into somebody else. Except she's still the same. Do you know something? When I kissed her, I could smell perfume. Underneath all that ether smell and shit like that, she'd like *put this perfume or cologne on!*"

146

Laurel has stopped in the middle of the sidewalk, and Jeffrey is pulling vaguely at her arm. "Come on," he says finally.

"God, nothing will ever change her! It's like it'll always be the same. There's this fantastic *innocence* about her, and yet . . . you know, she's still my like *mother!* Oh, God, it's no wonder my head is so fucked up!"

Jeffrey tugs at her arm, and she starts moving forward again in the direction of the bar where J. Dan is waiting for them.

Jeffrey feels lazy, out of it, weird. He wipes his hands largely through his hair, and then they both see their images crop up in the gun-metal-blue window of the Crazy Horse Bar and Grill. They slow down by consensus and instinct, and take in briefly their pre-faded, plaid-lined jeans, their oiled, natural steerhide cowboy boots, their heavy, new CPO's opened upon creamy wool, imported Irish sweaters.

But from this pulse of regard, they accelerate to the entrance of the Crazy Horse and push open the heavy stained-oak door into a warm, closed cave of metallic light, filled with beer fumes and booze currents, filigreed with cigarette and cigar smoke.

At a far booth, beyond the bar, sits J. Dan, a beer before him, his arms crossed, his body humped up against the back of the booth and the wall, and sound asleep. His hair is plastered neatly to the hard round knob of his head, and his jagged and grim lips are pulled almost apart by the sag of his jaw.

When they go over and sit down across the table from him, sliding into the booth, he doesn't move.

"J. Dan," Laurel whispers. Then louder: "J. Dan!"

Still he doesn't wake up, so she reaches across the table and around the beer and pats his arm. "J. Dan," she says louder, and his eyes come sadly open upon them.

"I fell asleep," he explains, rubbing his hand over his mouth. "Just came over me like a damn fit."

"You feel all right?" Laurel asks.

"Hundred per cent," J. Dan says. Then he picks up a camera

from the seat beside him and hands it to Jeffrey, saying, "Your damn picture-taking days are not exactly over, after all. I would like to ask you to take a picture of Laurel, along with her mother and me."

Jeffrey stares silently at the camera a moment, and then looks up at J. Dan and takes it.

"Unless you don't want to," J. Dan says. "In which case, I will get me a nurse or somebody to do the job."

Jeffrey shakes his head and says, "No, I'll do it."

"I never did take me the time to learn how to use one of them damn things right," J. Dan says. "But I expect you can handle it."

"Yes, I know how to use it," Jeffrey says in a faraway voice.

"Well then, our problems are solved," J. Dan says. "Now, you can order yourselves some damn drinks, and then we'll get us some lunch. But right now, I am going to go take me a leak."

J. Dan rises from the table, placing his hands against it and pushing solidly. The table does not jar, and the beer in his glass does not move at all.

"I suppose you've forgotten all that other film," Laurel says, staring at J. Dan's glass of beer.

A slender, white-haired waitress, with the name Rachel stenciled on her black uniform, comes up and asks them what they want, and they order two bottles of Coor's. When she leaves, Laurel asks, "Haven't you?"

"No," Jeffrey says.

Laurel turns and stares at him. "You've got to be kidding," she says.

"I have all the film I took," Jeffrey says. "Which should be enough. I mean, *more* than enough."

Laurel shakes her head and says, "I don't even begin to know what you're after."

"Maybe the words haven't been made yet," Jeffrey says. "But I know. I mean, I can feel it. It all has to be gotten down. *Then* we'll know."

The waitress returns with their beers; and then they see J. Dan stop by the bar, talk with her a minute, and pick up another beer for himself. When he gets back to the table, they all three sit in silence and drink pensively, each one wrapped up in his own thoughts.

After the waitress brings their lunch of open-faced tuna-fish sandwiches and salad, J. Dan says, "I called the doctor right before you two come in here, and when I asked him again, he said there wasn't no damn question but what she is dying and dying soon. He said she was clearheaded now, but that these things come in waves, and we just got here at the top of the wave. And there is no damn telling when she will go down again. But he said the next time will be it."

"I didn't realize she didn't like *know!*" Laurel cries, cutting into the open-faced sandwich with her knife and fork. Her hair collapses over her face as she starts sawing vigorously.

J. Dan stares at her a second, and then looks at Jeffrey, who catches his eye briefly, and then looks down at his sandwich.

"I mean," Laurel whispers, "it's so fucking *pathetic*. You know?" She swallows, and the act of swallowing seems to release tears that stream down her cheeks. She sniffs and says, "Oh, shit, I can't eat!"

"Drink the rest of your beer," J. Dan says. "It'll make you feel better."

"Oh, God!" Jeffrey cries in a soft voice, leaning his head back against the booth and looking up at the ceiling. "You people are too *much!* Don't you even know what you're *doing?*"

"It seems to me," J. Dan says, stuffing a thick wad of tuna fish and toast in his mouth, "that I have known what I was doing from the damn word go. Which is more than I could say for a lot of damn people."

Jeffrey starts to laugh, turning his head aside, and then sinks his head forward into both hands and nods his face up and down in it, so that it is uncertain whether he is crying or laughing.

"From what they say," J. Dan says studiously, "I would guess it might be tonight."

"Don't worry," Laurel hisses, her face still lowered over the sandwich. "We're not going to miss out on anything. We're staying until it's *all over* . . . until she like *isn't* any more!"

J. Dan nods and says, "It would be simpler if you stayed out there at the house; but if it makes you feel too bad, I'll put you both up in a motel."

"No," Laurel whispers at her plate, "none of that makes any difference now. One place isn't any different from another."

J. Dan nods and takes another large bite.

Jeffrey has stopped eating, and is holding the camera J. Dan gave him, studying it with great attention.

37 Her hair is fixed, and she is wearing her frilly pink robe that J. Dan bought her last Christmas. With help from the nurse and J. Dan, she is finally able to sit up in bed, packed against the two pillows, her head half dangling like an enormous, overripe bud. Her smile is an expression of pain and delirium, and possibly of a dim self-consciousness in having her picture taken.

The nurse stands aside, and then opens the Venetian blinds, letting slats of light fall weightlessly across the foot of the bed.

The room is crowded with their bodies and still smells of hay and medication and morbidity. There is no perceptible odor of perfume.

Laurel moves over to one side of the bed, propping up her mother's wasted body, and J. Dan stands on the other side. They are both looking at Jeffrey, who is standing by the door with the camera.

"Lean in a little closer to one another," Jeffrey says.

"My family," Florence whispers. "Oh, God, at *last!*"

"Don't keep her sitting up like that too long," the nurse says.

"I'm all right," Florence protests in a weak voice. And then, taking a strong breath and with a great effort she opens her eyes all the way and smiles brightly at the camera.

There is a soft pulse of light, and J. Dan starts counting, "One thousand one, one thousand two, one thousand three . . ." and then continues silently, as the nurse comes over to the bed and eases Florence back into a supine position.

"Now it's ready," J. Dan says.

"What are you talking about?" Jeffrey asks. "This isn't a Polaroid camera."

J. Dan blinks twice and then says, "Well, they all look the same to me. Like I told you, I don't know nothing about cameras, and never did!"

"That's all right," Florence whispers. "Just so we got a picture."

"Take another one," J. Dan says. "To make sure."

"That was the last one on the film," Jeffrey says.

"I should have got me some more damn film," J. Dan states, shaking his head in disgust. "I should have thought ahead."

"That's all right," Florence mutters, but no one understands what she has said, and when Laurel asks her, she doesn't repeat it.

"I thought it was a damn Polaroid," J. Dan whispers, leaning over toward Jeffrey.

Florence drifts off, her eyebrows raised delicately and her eyes closed; the expression on her face is almost smiling, like that of an infant suffering from gas pains.

Laurel steps softly over to the two men and, looking up at J. Dan, says, "She *does* know, doesn't she?"

J. Dan nods, looking at the window. "She has known for a damn year," he says.

151

38 The ranch house was a dumpy, two-story, gray shingle building, standing in isolation beside the road, with two sheds, a little horse barn, and a windmill for company.

J. Dan used to point out to her, in his slow, stupid-sounding voice, that you could see the lights from town reflected in the sky on a clear night; but that was small comfort to Laurel at the age of sixteen, and she soon learned to despise him for even making an attempt to comfort her.

The house had a little kitchen at the rear, and standing there washing or drying the dishes, Laurel would stare out at the windmill and the big boxlike wooden pen that J. Dan would fix on the back of his pickup for his two greyhounds, Scratch and Stranger, when he went out for coyotes. He owned four sections of land; and she learned to hate every cold, windy, barren acre, along with all the stupid wall-eyed cattle.

When they came in, J. Dan turned on the television set, which was showing a shaky black-and-white rerun of an old *F Troop* show, in which comic Indians and an inept U.S. Cavalry unit parodied the winning of the West.

Without asking, J. Dan poured bourbon and water for all of them, and they spent an hour and a half sitting in front of the set, silently getting drunk like patrons in a dark and shabby bar.

Finally, Laurel stumbled out to the kitchen and scrambled some eggs for them, mixing onions, cheese, and pepper in the frying pan as she focused first one eye and then the other, to see what she was doing. Jeffrey came out a few minutes later and put the coffeepot on, and then Laurel made toast and fried some hash browns.

"They don't have any bacon," she said to no one in particular. "And no sausage or steak." She started breathing heavily.

"It doesn't make any difference," Jeffrey said, leaning back against the counter and drinking.

Between the sounds of a Tums commercial in the front room, they heard J. Dan snoring.

"I would have liked a good steak," Laurel said. "I mean, it's just like him not to have steak in. Mother fries him one just about every day. Or used to."

"It doesn't make any damn difference," Jeffrey said distantly, his eyes half closed.

He swirled his drink, and Laurel said, "Thank God we won't have to be here like very *long!*"

"I know," Jeffrey said, and drank.

The wind picked up and whirred at the eaves by the kitchen. Hearing it, Jeffrey turned around and stared out upon absolute blackness.

"You can't see a single light anywhere," Jeffrey said.

"I know," Laurel said. "That's because there isn't anything out there. Anywhere. Nothing between here and Denver, two hundred fucking, impossible, Godforsaken miles away. It's like *no wonder* I can't get myself together, is it?"

In the front room, J. Dan swallowed a snore and woke up. Then, realizing where he was and who was with him, he turned back on the sofa and went to sleep again.

Both of the greyhounds, which J. Dan had let in when they came into the house, sat at the edge of the kitchen and waited for handouts. Laurel stared at them drunkenly, and pushed her hair out of her face with her hand.

"God, I'm hot in this sweater," she said. "J. Dan always did keep the house too hot. And Mother."

"Where's the dog food?" Jeffrey asked. "I'll feed the dogs."

"Feed the puppy, too," Laurel said. And as if hearing her, the puppy waddled into the kitchen and looked up at her in the yellow light.

"We haven't even named him yet," Laurel commented sadly, as if they had wronged him in neglecting such a thing. "The greyhounds are named Scratch and Stranger."

"I said, where's the dog food?" Jeffrey said.

"Oh," Laurel said, frowning. "Under the sink. Here. Right here." She opened the cabinet under the sink, and pulled out a twenty-five-pound sack of dog food, skidding it on the linoleum.

Jeffrey poured it out into two bowls, while Laurel filled a saucer with milk. She sniffed it to see if it was sour, and then put it on the floor in front of the puppy.

"We've got to like give him a *name*," she said.

"The name will wait," Jeffrey said.

They stood there without speaking, and watched the two greyhounds and the puppy eat.

When the greyhounds finished, Laurel went over, opened the door, and snapped her fingers. "All right, Scratch and Stranger, out!" she cried, and the dogs slunk out quickly, with rounded backs and heads down.

"Lucifer," Jeffrey said.

"What?"

"That's what we'll name him."

Laurel studied the dog with a solemn, drunken expression. He had trotted over to the refrigerator and was reaching under the edge, trying to dislodge a small gray piece of bread. The refrigerator went on, and the sudden humming noise startled the puppy, making him jump back.

Jeffrey and Laurel both started to laugh, and then they stopped when they saw J. Dan standing in the entranceway to the front room.

"I am about ready," he said, "to have me some damn dinner."

"Some damn dinner coming up," Laurel said recklessly, sliding the frying pan off the stove, onto the dirty counter next to it. With a clatter, she got out some plates, and Jeffrey poured the coffee, spilling some on the bare oak table.

"Right there on the table," Laurel said, nodding to the little breakfast nook where it seemed she had eaten ten thousand meals. "Oh, I guess we've set the table, haven't we?"

"One of us ought to call to see how she is," J. Dan said, pouring himself a water glass half full of whiskey. He went to the refrigerator, got out the ice-cube tray, and plopped two cubes in the glass. Then he filled it with water.

"You drink whiskey like it's going out of style," Laurel said. Then she paused in a moment's confusion, realizing that she had heard her mother say the same thing to J. Dan a hundred times.

But J. Dan nodded, and sipped from the glass.

"We've named him Lucifer," Laurel said.

"The little pup?" J. Dan asked.

"The very same. It's a beautiful name for a beautiful beast."

"Damn Heinz dog."

"He's his own thoroughbred, and nobody else's."

Suddenly, the meal was on the table, and they all stood looking at it as if it had appeared there by magic.

"Well," Laurel said. "I mean, shit, let's eat."

When they sat down, Jeffrey said in a solemn voice, "Lord, bless this food and make us happy and wise."

Both Laurel and J. Dan looked at him in muted, drunken surprise, and then began to eat . . . identically, as if it were their last meal on earth.

39 Badly hung over, J. Dan put on his faded-brown terry-cloth bathrobe, phoned the hospital next morning at 7:25, and learned that Florence Burch had died during the night.

He went into the kitchen and drank a beer, and then vomited in the sink, before he could even get to the bathroom. He turned the hot-water faucet on and then staggered over to the door and opened it. A cold winter wind from the empty land flowed in upon him, immersing his body in frigid air. The two greyhounds came running inside and nuzzled against his bare legs.

"Somebody left them outside all night," J. Dan said. Then he sat down at the kitchen table, leaned over, and buried his head in his hands. The floor seemed to drift underneath him, and there were icy ants and flies crawling all over his body under the robe.

With a shudder, he dislodged them and turned around to see Laurel standing in the doorway, fully dressed.

"Well?" she said. "Why did you leave the water running in the sink?"

"It is all over," J. Dan said. "Now you are all I have got left in the whole damn world."

When Laurel didn't say anything, J. Dan muttered, "God, I wish I was dead my own self."

"J. Dan," Laurel said, turning away from him and going over to the sink, "don't be such an ass hole." She turned the water off.

He raised his head and stared at her as she filled the coffeepot and then began to shovel big, slopping scoops from the Maxwell House can into it. Her face was pale and expressionless. Her arms and hands worked with an abstract energy, spilling coffee grounds all over.

J. Dan sat there in a nimbus of misery while she prepared breakfast. A few minutes later, Jeffrey came and stood in the doorway, rubbing the back of his neck with his eyes closed.

"Wow," he said. "Wow!"

J. Dan turned away from him and stared out across his land. "I would like to have her buried out there," he said. "And I'd like to be lying out there beside her."

"Oh, shut the fuck up!" Laurel said.

"What's the matter?" Jeffrey asked, taking two steps into the kitchen. The puppy followed him.

"Oh, there's Lucifer!" Laurel said, her lips in a kissing expression. She didn't stop what she was doing, but cast an ardent glance at the puppy as it sat down and scratched its muzzle with its hind foot.

"Is she dead?" Jeffrey asked.

"Yes," Laurel said. "He said she died last night. But I mean, it's like we *knew* it, didn't we?"

"Sure. I guess we did."

J. Dan got up from his chair and said, "I am going to have me a hair of the damn dog."

"Drink all you want," Laurel said, "only, don't pass up breakfast. Do you hear? J. Dan! Do you hear?"

"I hear," J. Dan said.

"Then you can kill yourself on a full stomach."

"I hear," J. Dan repeated.

"Christ, *men!*" Laurel whispered, and started to dish out the fried eggs and hash browns.

Laurel turned on the radio, and then they sat down and ate silently, not looking at one another.

When he was finished, J. Dan stood up and said, "Well, I have got me a thousand damn things to do."

"J. Dan," Laurel said, "you look like shit warmed over."

J. Dan nodded and said, "And that is just about the exact way I feel."

He went out of the kitchen into the front room and got his coat on. When he came back, he said, "I'll give you two a ride into town, if that's what you want. I am going to be gone all day, arranging for the funeral and trying to get the damn transmission fixed if I can. Also, I have got me a dozen damn *other* things to take care of."

"I think it's real sweet," Laurel said, "that you can think of getting the transmission fixed at a time like this!"

"Don't be sarcastic," J. Dan said.

"What do you *expect* me to be!" Laurel shrieked. "My mother dies and all you can think of is that fucking pickup!"

J. Dan wiped his hand over his eyes and said, "Well, what else *is* there for a man to do?"

"Don't let her hassle you, J. Dan," Jeffrey said.

Both of them turned to look at him, and then J. Dan nodded and said, "Well, I'll be seeing you."

He went out the front door and got in the pickup. It didn't start easily, because of the chilled engine, but finally it was turning over, and J. Dan twisted around in his seat, looking back as he eased it out of the damn driveway, up onto the gravel road.

The wind bucked against it twice before he started accelerating toward town.

"Winter," J. Dan said, as if someone were there to hear him.

40 Bill Banks was a short, stocky man with an unnaturally large head and a white mustache and goatee. He looked a little like Buffalo Bill reflected in a fun-house mirror, all squashed up. He always wore expensive, tooled cowboy boots, which brought his height up a little nearer to man-sized. His eyes were deep-set and gray, and his voice was a resonant bass. A retired agricultural agent, he lived six miles farther out of town than J. Dan, with his wife and their crippled thirty-two-year-old daughter. This was the place where J. Dan and five other men met once a week to play poker, and tell lies and old stories and dirty jokes, and get a little drunk on quarts of beer.

During the day, Bill Banks spent a lot of time in town, at the Crazy Horse Bar and Grill during the hours before they closed the drapes and Venetian blinds and sealed off the interior for the evening trade. He liked to sit at one of the window seats and drink coffee until noon, playing solitaire and kidding everybody within earshot. He was a good friend of the owner, and his rumbling bass voice was familiar to everyone in town.

When J. Dan came in, Bill Banks said, "I was sure sorry to hear the bad news, J. Dan. Come over here and let me buy you a damn drink."

J. Dan nodded and joined him in the booth.

"She died last night," he said.

"That's what I heard," Bill Banks said. He looked down at the cards before him as if he couldn't quite recognize what they were. He raised his eyebrows and sighed.

"And I am hung over so bad," J. Dan said, "that I would have to raise my head to look a damn *cat* in the eye!"

Bill Banks chuckled briefly at J. Dan's familiar joke, but then called out, "Rachel, bring J. Dan here a hair of the damn dog!"

"What are you drinking, J. Dan?" Rachel said, coming over to the table and wiping her hands on a gray cloth.

"Oh, bourbon and water will be fine."

"How about a Bloody Mary?" Rachel said. She was a pretty woman, with one eye closed in a permanent half-wink and black combs in her white hair.

"Sure," J. Dan said. "That'll be better."

"Vitamin B in the tomato juice," Bill Banks said, slapping a red nine down on a ten of clubs.

"I'm sorry to hear about Florence," Rachel said. "But I guess it didn't come as no surprise, did it?"

"No, it didn't," J. Dan said.

"Well, at least her suffering is over, the poor woman."

"That's the truth," J. Dan said.

"Have you had yourself some breakfast?" Bill Banks asked.

J. Dan nodded.

"You don't want to make yourself sick," the other man said judiciously, slapping the queen of clubs down on top of the king of hearts.

"No, although the damn truth is, I couldn't be much worse off than I feel right now," J. Dan said lugubriously, staring out the window at the cold gray light of day.

41 Bill pulls his pickup into J. Dan's driveway, and says, "Well, J. Dan, we made it."

The greyhounds are beside the car, barking. J. Dan nods; then opens the door and eases a gob of chewing tobacco out onto the ground, just missing Stranger as he jumps back. "Come on in, and I'll give you a damn drink."

"Is Laurel in there?"

"Yes, with her boy friend. The one I told you about, that come all the way with us and was always taking pictures with his damn *movie* camera."

Bill Banks nods. Both men are a little drunk.

"I should have taken the damn Plymouth Kiely offered me until the pickup's fixed."

"No," Bill Banks says. "Like I told you, I don't have me nothing else to do in the whole world, and I'll take you wherever you want. *Anywhere*, J. Dan."

"Well, come on in and have a drink."

"Why don't you and both of the kids come over to my house, and I'll have Charlotte cook us up some steaks."

"Come on in, and we'll talk about it in there," J. Dan says, getting out of the pickup and kicking one of the dogs aside.

It is late afternoon, almost evening, and on the dim silver sod the shadows lie long and vague, formed by the dirty gray sunlight shining generally out of the western sky. The wind has lessened, but it is still cold, and the air smells a little like copper.

When J. Dan opens the door, he calls out to them, but there is no answer. Bill Banks comes in and, breathing heavily, sits down on the sofa with his jacket still on.

J. Dan goes all through the house, calling out for them. When he returns to the front room, he says, "They're not here. They're gone."

"Maybe they just went into town," Bill Banks says.

J. Dan nods and rubs his hand over his eyes. Then he goes to the back door and lets the greyhounds in. "Bourbon?" he calls out, and Bill Banks says, "Well, I guess I could take one. Make it light, though. I'm seeing double already, and soon to see triple."

J. Dan cracks the ice-cube trays open and splashes Old Charter from a fifth into a couple of water glasses. After he puts

160

the ice-cube trays back in the refrigerator and goes over to run some water in the glasses, he sees a freshly baked cake on the counter, with a folded sheet of paper sticking out from under the plate it's sitting on.

He takes the paper out, unfolds it, and reads the following:

J. Dan:

Guess what? I remembered where Mother kept her jewelry upstairs in the back of one of the dresser drawers so I liberated it, and to the joy of all concerned (i.e., Jeffrey and me) found the pearl necklace you got her, along with a couple of bracelets and rings—several hundred dollars worth of things that I guess belong to me anyway. If we sell this stuff in town it will be more than enough to get us back to Wichita by bus (but then we may hitchhike, in case you get some crazy idea about following us). Not only that, I've got some money too. So, "Mission Completed," as they say.

I mean, you got what you wanted, and you were right (for this I'm glad), and I got to see Mother and say good-by to her (practically, anyway). Neither Jeffrey nor I have any feeling for the shitty, dismal burial rites that will follow, so this is it.

J. Dan, you've got to know that I loved Mother. I mean, I really did! There, I've said it. But I pitied her, too; and no matter how fucked up in the head you think I've been the past couple of days, I know what I'm doing. As a matter of fact, I feel pity for you, too . . . so much pity, if you must know (and like all of a sudden), that it's almost like love. I mean, I really can't explain it. But the truth is, I couldn't stand the thought of being around you much longer (maybe because of this). Anyway, this is good-by.

Honest to God, as long as I live, I'll never forget that fantastic trip! I mean, when I think of a tornado forming right above our three heads, I get goose bumps all over my arms. You know? It's like the finger of God or something. (But that sounds the way Jeffrey's beginning to sound, and he may not know it, but he's only about two degrees off from being a Jesus freak.) (Incidentally, Jeffrey will read this, but as you probably know, I'm not about to take any shit from him or from any other man.)

Good luck to you, J. Dan. Keep your pecker up. (Or get it up, or something.)

Laurel

P.S. We're taking Lucifer with us, of course. He peed on the stairway rug straining himself to climb the steps and like join us while Jeffrey and I were making out in yours and Mother's bed. Third step from the top. I cleaned it up a little, but it might smell in a day or two. No more time, Jeffrey says. It is ten after three.

L.

P.P.S. Oh yes, in case you haven't guessed, this raisin cake is for you. I remember you used to like them, and maybe you'll remember that sometimes I used to help Mother bake them for you. Also, that I do like to do nice things for people. (All right, Jeffrey, I'm coming!)

L. (again)

P.P.P.S. SAY GOOD-BY TO BETTY BUMP, J. DAN. AND IF YOU'D LIKE TO KNOW, <u>YOU WIN</u>.

J.

He finished the letter and shook his head slowly.

"What all are you doing in there, J. Dan?" Bill Banks asked from the front room.

"I'll be there in a minute," J. Dan said. He picked up the two bourbons, walked into the front room, put one down on the coffee table before Bill Banks, and then turned on the television.

There was an old Jimmy Stewart movie on, so J. Dan turned the volume low and went over to his special chair and sat down. The two men sat there drinking silently and watching the set for a few minutes.

When he finished the drink, J. Dan was really drunk. He ambled out to the kitchen, tripping over one of the greyhounds, and kicking at it with a brief, halfhearted curse. He poured more bourbon into his glass and called out to Bill Banks, asking if he wanted more.

"Hell no," Bill Banks said. "I'm damn near stupefied as it is. Charlotte will raise hell if I get any drunker. Shit, I can't hardly hold my head up as it *is!*"

J. Dan nodded and said, "Well, nobody's around to hassle *me* no more, I guess." He took a drink, and then staggered as he looked at the cake.

"Look here, Bill," he called.

"What is it?" Bill Banks answered without moving from the sofa.

"She baked a damn cake."

Bill Banks sighed, got up, and came into the kitchen. He stood there for an instant, and then scratched his shoulder so hard, it seemed to shove his own body aside, and he staggered a little and blinked out at what J. Dan was holding in his hands.

"A damn raisin cake," J. Dan said.

"Laurel did that?"

"That's right. She baked it," J. Dan said.

Bill Banks nodded and walked over to the back door. "Charlotte's going to raise hell. She's worried about my blood pressure."

"Wait a minute," J. Dan said. "Just hold the hell on."

"What is it?"

"You know something? I've got me a damn suspicion."

"Like what?"

J. Dan rubbed the back of his neck and frowned. "I am not going to take me a bite of that cake. You know why?"

"Why?"

"Because that girl is capable of any damn thing. She is capable of putting LSD in a damn cake."

"I'll be damned," Bill Banks said, sitting down in one of the kitchen chairs with his knees sagging apart.

"I wouldn't be surprised at all," J. Dan said.

"*I* would," Bill Banks said, nodding.

Then J. Dan snapped his fingers and said, "I've got it."

"What?"

J. Dan lifted the cake up and carried it over to the dogs' bowls, and scooped a handful of the cake into each bowl, scattering some on the floor. When he stepped back, he bumped into the refrigerator.

The two greyhounds began chomping it down, and Bill Banks said, "It won't hurt them, will it? I mean, if it's got LSD in it?"

"No," J. Dan said, "because how could one of them damn hallucinations make any difference to a *dog*?"

Bill Banks nodded and said, "Damned if I know!"

"We'll keep our eye on them, though."

Breathing heavily, both men watched the two dogs eat the cake. Then they continued watching them after they'd finished, so that the dogs became uneasy. Stranger lay down with his head in his paws and whined at them. Scratch got under the table and just stood there, looking out.

"They *seem* to be okay," Bill Banks said tentatively. "As near as I can tell, what with all this damn booze in me. Only it wouldn't have any effect this early, would it?"

"Damned if I know," J. Dan said.

Stranger jumped to his feet and turned around in a nervous circle.

"Look at that!" Bill Banks whispered.

"Hell," J. Dan said, "Stranger's just nervous from us watching him so damn close."

"Well, let's go in the other room and leave them alone."

J. Dan nodded, and when they left, Scratch followed at their heels, whining softly. The Jimmy Stewart movie had been interrupted for a Plymouth commercial.

"I should have taken that damn Plymouth from Kiely," J. Dan said lugubriously. "A man likes to have himself some damn transportation."

"Listen, I'll take you anywhere you want to go," Bill Banks said. "No problem. That's what friends are for. Anywhere, J. Dan."

J. Dan got up and went into the kitchen, checking on Stranger, who whined when he saw him.

"Is he high?" Bill Banks called out from the other room. "Is he stoned?"

"No," J. Dan said. "I don't think so. He's just nervous. He knows something is up, for me to check up on him like this."

"I thought maybe he was high," Bill Banks said, sighing, and lying back against the arm of the sofa. He closed first one eye and then the other as he tried to focus the Jimmy Stewart movie. Jimmy Stewart was standing with his hands spread wide apart, trying to explain something to a young woman with long pale hair and dark lips. She didn't believe what he was saying, and yet it was obvious that she loved him anyway. Her dress reached almost to her ankles.

"The dogs seem to be okay," J. Dan said, coming back into the front room. "I wouldn't have given them the damn cake if I thought there was a serious risk. Some dogs I like better than people."

"Me too," Bill Banks said.

"Of course, you can never tell. That girl is capable of doing *any* damn thing. Always was. Her mother couldn't do a damn thing with her!"

"She always was a headstrong girl, I remember," Bill Banks said.

J. Dan nodded, and then he felt sick at his stomach and went into the bathroom and vomited.

When he came staggering out a few minutes later, Bill Banks was asleep on the sofa, and the two greyhounds were standing there looking at him nervously, wanting to get out. Apparently there was nothing wrong with them that the fresh air and open ground wouldn't cure. At least, so far there wasn't.

J. Dan nodded, went to the back door and opened it for them. He watched them as they bounded out into the cold, windy twilight.

"I've got to get me some damn feed for the cattle," J. Dan said, half aloud. He got himself a glass of water and drank it straight down. Then he drank another glass of water just as quickly.

When he went into the front room, he woke up Bill Banks and told him he'd better get home or Charlotte would sure as hell scalp him alive. She'd be worried about him. Bill nodded and said J. Dan had better come along and have some dinner with him.

"No, I will be all right," J. Dan said.

Bill nodded and blinked heavily, seeming to listen long after J. Dan had stopped speaking. Then he got on his jacket, walked slowly outside, climbed into his pickup, and drove cautiously up the road in the direction of his place.

J. Dan returned to the house and stood for a minute by the sink in back, looking for the dogs. But they weren't in sight, so he went back into the front room.

Then he remembered something: the roll of film he had taken in to have developed the day before, with a special hurry-up order on it to have prints by today. He went to the phone and called the photo-supply store where he'd left the film. Nobody answered, and he realized that they had closed for the day.

He sat down in front of the television and watched a while; then he climbed up the stairs to bed, not even bothering to turn the damn thing off. The realization that the pickup wasn't outside made him vaguely uneasy.

He slept fitfully, dreaming in scratchy black and white about a man whose adventures were disconnected, unreal, and without point. The man walked around in strange places, with windmills standing close together like fence posts on the horizon. A Styrofoam sky stretched like a lumpy ceiling overhead, and a casket was being lowered into the earth.

It was Florence, of course.

Nothing had shape. Nothing led anywhere. The simplest things in the dream were hideous with clarity, cruel with a poisonous emanation that made the gray air stink, so that one died constantly and was never dead. Without fulfillment. Inconsequent.

Laurel was walking away from him, and Jeffrey was calling him "Daddy," and then laughing in his face.

Always dying, never dead. Always leaving, never there.

At Lawson's Funeral Home, J. Dan stood alone by the entrance. Someone had left the windows open, and the cold wind blew everything in the room—the tassels on the old-fashioned cloth table covers, the curtains, the Venetian-blind cords, the pages in the big Bible on the walnut stand . . . even the pages in the visitors' book resting on an identical stand.

J. Dan signed his name, and the wind blew the page over. He signed again, and the same thing happened. He leaned over on the book with his elbow and signed slowly and heavily, and then the pages began to blow through his arm, turning, turning, turning, erasing the one that had gone before and constantly being replaced by the next, so that they flowed like water before his eyes and flipped like meaningless cards in a badly lighted viewer, smelling of old nickel and brass, in a penny arcade.

42 "I thought she was going to have herself a shit hemorrhage," Bill Banks says, taking a sip from his coffee cup. He puts the cup down and shakes his head. "*Damn* if I didn't!" He chuckles in his deep, rumbling bass and then starts coughing.

"I am a little bit hung over my *damn* self," J. Dan states, scratching the back of his neck and gazing out upon the interior landscape of the Crazy Horse Bar and Grill. He sees Rachel carrying a Bloody Mary toward him, and he watches her until she places it on the table before him. "In fact," he says, "I would have to lift my damn head to look a cat in the eye."

Bill Banks nods and says, "Charlotte said to me this morning, 'Why do you have to kill yourself, you dumbbell?' Know what I said?"

"No," J. Dan answers, sipping from his Bloody Mary.

"I said, 'What difference will it make a hundred years from now? And not only that, what *else* is there for me to do?' "

J. Dan nods and sips again.

"That stumped her," Bill Banks says, nodding and putting the three of diamonds on the four of clubs. "Thoroughly stumped her ass. She didn't have herself an answer for *that* one, J. Dan. Because there *wasn't* any answer, that's why. There never *is!*"

"That hair of the damn dog," J. Dan says, "makes me feel a little bit better. That was something I needed."

"Not that Charlotte isn't a good old girl. By God, she'd *have* to be to stay married to *me* for forty years!" Bill Banks rumbles a laugh, and then slowly waves the jack of diamonds over his cards, looking for a black queen.

"You must have sniffed that one up through the nose," Rachel says, appearing suddenly at J. Dan's side and picking up his glass.

"Looks like it evaporated. Give me another one just like it."

"Now I remember what I wanted to ask you," Bill Banks says, lifting his eyes toward J. Dan. "How are those two dogs of yours? They okay? They having themselves any symptoms of any kind?"

"No, they're both okay," J. Dan says. "There wasn't any damn thing in that raisin cake, after all."

Bill Banks nods, and then lifts his eyebrows when he uncovers a black ace.

"There could have been though," J. Dan says.

"Sure."

"I mean, you can't have any damn *idea* of what those two kids were like, Bill! You'd have to see it to believe it."

"Kids these days are sure messed up. Makes me glad I'm not one of them."

"Yes," J. Dan explains, "but there's more to it than that."

"What do you mean?"

"I mean, it's more than them being messed up. That time on the road with them two really taught me something: they just don't speak the same language as you and I do, Bill."

Bill Banks nods and finishes the game with the three of hearts on the four of spades. He picks up the deck and shuffles it slowly in his hands, gazing out through the open Venetian blinds into the cold sunlight.

"Cattlemen warnings are out," he says. "Your stock all right?"

"I've got them all in the south section next to the road," J. Dan says comfortably. "So everything is taken care of."

"J. Dan," Bill Banks says, starting to lay his cards down for another game of solitaire, "you look tired. That trip must have taken a lot out of you."

"Not to mention the damn whiskey," J. Dan says, rubbing the palm of his hand over his eyes. Then he picks up the Bloody Mary and takes another sip.

"Who's taking care of the funeral?" Bill Banks asks. "Lawson's?"

"That's who I called," J. Dan says.

"When you get to be our age, there's more people you've known who are dead than are living."

J. Dan raises his eyes and looks at the old man across from him. But Bill Banks doesn't seem to be aware that he has said anything out of the ordinary, and simply lays two cards down in rapid succession, and then pushes his almost-empty coffee cup aside to give him more room.

"It was still the right thing to do," J. Dan says. "I mean, for her to come here to say good-by to her mother."

"Why, of course it was."

"I'll tell you, she was really surprised, too."

"Florence was?"

"That's right. Even down underneath all them drugs and things they give her, you could kind of see her eyes light up. You know?"

"Sure. I'll bet she *was* glad to see Laurel."

"She never figured she would ever see her again."

"No, I'll bet she didn't."

J. Dan reaches inside his pocket and pulls out a yellow package filled with photographic prints. He sorts through them, picks out one and passes it across the table to Bill Banks.

The other man takes the picture and tilts his face back to stare at it. Then he reaches over on the seat beside him and picks up a pair of horn-rimmed glasses. "I need these cheaters on for close-up work," he says.

Then he looks at the photograph. It shows Florence sitting up in bed, with Laurel leaning over on one side, and J. Dan on the other. All three are facing the camera; only, at the instant of exposure, Florence had blinked and her eyes are closed, so she already looks like a corpse. Laurel's hair has fallen down, obscuring one side of her face, but as well as one can tell, her expression is vague, and she looks very young. J. Dan's expression is blank, as usual, only he looks very old, tired, and a little angry.

"Are there any other pictures of the three of you together?" Bill Banks asks.

"No, that is it," J. Dan answers. "There was only one picture left in the camera. If I had known it, I would have gotten another damn roll of film."

"How's come she has her eyes closed? Florence, I mean. Her eyes are closed."

"I guess she blinked right when the picture was taken," J. Dan says, studying the photograph.

Bill Banks looks up at J. Dan, a little surprised by the tone in his voice. He hands the photograph back to him and says, "Will you be okay, J. Dan?"

J. Dan nods and says, "I will be all right as soon as I can get ahold of myself, and get back to my stock and take care of them properly." He pauses, sips his Bloody Mary slowly, and then looks out the window through the Venetian blinds into the daylight. "And get back on my damn feet, and get me some sleep. And forget about them two and the damn trip we had together."

43 They had boarded the Greyhound over an hour ago, Laurel wearing her knapsack, and then taking it off and shoving it in the carrier overhead, her CPO flapping open, her heavy breasts swaying with her vigorous tugs and pushes, and her hair flying all about as she nodded her head and grunted with effort. The knapsack didn't want to fit, but Laurel jammed until the damn thing fit anyway, and then sat down beside him, red-faced and panting, and licking her lips.

Then they were retracing the same route, seeing everything in reversed sequence—the backs of signs and buildings that had flashed their surfaces mutely only two days before.

"I'll never be the same," Laurel whispered out of nowhere to the back of the seat ahead.

"Nobody will," Jeffrey said.

He yawned, at the moment unimpressed by her melodramatic bulletins, and watched the landscape move by . . . seeing the flow of images as a living film that travelers experienced. Only here, the images were minimal, and Jeffrey thought of the flow in terms of the maximal laconism he wanted.

No, that wasn't it, either.

Laurel fell asleep with her head thrown back and her lips parted. Her mouth was puckered a little, as if she were trying to whistle.

The bus was only a third full, and it lumbered forward, warm and purposeful. There was a smell of peppermint in the air from

171

the two girls up ahead who were chewing gum and reading paperbacks—both of them together, turning pages in counterpoint—each one inhabiting an independent life that was unfolding in her particular book.

Jeffrey half dozed, meditating. Then he took out his notebook and wrote:

THE BURGEONING ESS.

STILL PHOTO, UR-PHOTO, AT HEART OF.

SLOW SHOTS LIKE VIEWER IN PENNY ARCADE.

DAY, NIGHT FLASH TOGETHER.

TELEOLOGICAL PRESENCE IN EVERY CELL.

J. DAN STRIVES TO PERPETUATE HIMSELF, OR FOCUS OF HIS PIETAS, IN ACT OF VANISHING. THUS BECOMES GHOST. SEE TREES AND WINDMILLS ON HORIZON SHOWING THROUGH HIS KNEES AND THIGHS.

J. DAN AS HERO.

Impatiently, he closed the notebook, shoved it under his seat, and stared out the window. It seemed overwhelmingly evident, at the moment, that this film, *his* film, would never be made, would never become, would never show. This movie would never move.

Something was missing, or perhaps many things were missing. The long, flat, gray-and-tan vistas glided almost imperceptibly past the window, pulsing before his eyes, punctuated by the frenetic flick of fence posts and telephone poles in the foreground.

Maybe he would never make a film. Maybe all his brilliance, admired by teachers and professors for years, would flicker out in pathetic and ephemeral little dreams . . . ephemeral *little* dreams, rather than the ephemeral great ones that would be pictured forth in Plato's caves throughout the country, throughout the world, in that shared hallucination that the artist imposes upon the world, vindictively and egotistically, to become (no matter *how* ephemerally) *their* dream, too.

"Oh, shit," Laurel said distinctly.

In surprise, Jeffrey glanced at her and saw that she was still soundly asleep, locked in her own little dream, but pausing long enough to speak outside it and utter the words aloud, unequivocally, speaking in what he had once called Laurellian Burchese. But she had not laughed at the expression, merely frowned and said, "Cut out the crap." Q.E.D.

But now she was running up some down escalator, and even whimpering faintly. Some enormous J. Dan was chasing her and trying to make her behave.

"No," she said.

"Wake up," Jeffrey said, shaking her arm a little.

Laurel inhaled sharply and then twisted around, so that her breath blew toward him. It smelled faintly of stale cigarettes. Her eyes were still tightly closed. But in turning around, the edge of a piece of paper was squeezed out of her CPO pocket.

Jeffrey pulled it out and unfolded it. It was a song, crudely dittoed, and he recognized it as Peter Peters' last song, which Laurel had told him about, saying it was fantastic.

At the ranch house she had insisted on reading it to him, but he had only half listened. Now, however, he read the words carefully, thinking in his tiredness and discouragement that this might be part of the total eventing; and something of the eventual film might still be alive, nuzzling out of the darkness in search of the light on the screen. He thought for a moment, and then read it again:

> I ain't never going nowhere I ain't been.
> I been to Pittsburgh, Philly, and L.A.
> But all it ever brought me was a dish of sin,
> Heartburn, and a movie star's toupee.

> I'm sick of Jackie, Pat, and Mamie, everyone.
> They don't remember Peters, not at all.
> They think they'll get me with a cold steel gun.
> But they don't know the Vision that I saw.

I ain't never going nowhere I ain't been.
I been to Boston, Lauderdale, and Mobile.
But all it ever brought me was a shifty grin,
A fever to be gone, toothache, and a chill.

Old Peters, he'll be with you from now on.
He's thumbing west from Santa Fe today.
He'll get a ride back east from San Anton.
Man, you can't hide from Peters *any* way!

I ain't never going nowhere I ain't been.
I been to Butte and Fargo and Detroit.
But all it ever brought me was a pint of gin,
Salvation Army clothes, and electric light.

Man, it's going to be all different from now on.
That light you see ashining ain't no bulb.
It is the poet sun that writes the dawn.
You can hear it every morning, read by God.

After he tucked the paper back into Laurel's pocket, Jeffrey took up his notebook again. But then, before printing anything in it, he paused and brooded. If you look hard enough for something, you're sure to see it. Of course.

He looked at the woman sleeping beside him and realized what a marvel she was. She was blowing her breath on him, giving him something even while she was asleep.

But then that was crap, too—as she would be the first to point out. Still, she didn't know everything, and didn't understand much more. Vaguely, he reached over and rubbed her stomach, and she said, "Don't," and turned away, not even opening her eyes.

But in spite of all the internal warnings, expressions of that ferociously critical mind he had been developing, or trying to develop, all these years, Jeffrey was forced to consider that, somehow, Peter Peters' song was about eventing, and that the bulb was the projector bulb, conveying the film as construct, as artifact—it was the projector bulb, rather than the native sun, which must eventually prove their salvation.

Almost uneasily, he half expected to hear her say, "Bullshit"; but of course she was silent now, except for a distant, stertorous breathing from sleeping cramped up in a slanted seat, as she blew out into the warm aisle and dreamed of other things.

The quiet insistent movement of the bus was soporific; one of the girls up ahead had fallen asleep, while the other still held her paperback up in front of her face, making *that* her reality, rather than the equally fictitious, or structured, flow of landscape or the events in the bus.

Jeffrey stared at Laurel's cheekbone an instant, wondering at the enviable self-possession of those who sleep in public places, and then he turned his head back to the window, seeing the vague adumbration of his own features looking back, and—beyond that—the gliding swell and fall of prairie.

Before long, he was half dreaming, forgetful of his part in the eventual film, and hearing Peter Peters' last song as he might sing it to the accompaniment of his guitar.

J. Dan was frowning, leaning over and trying to uncurl the fingers of his own damn hand.

J. Dan, walking through a storm of conceptions that burst upon him like rain.

Then there were the two long, dark funnels trailing softly and silently over the land toward Maxton.

Then there were his own words: TELEOLOGICAL PATTERN CONTRA LITERAL SEQUENCE.

Then there was Peter Peters' sun, an enormous electric bulb that would not burn out within our memory, and would not be switched off.

He couldn't forget the little shithead, no matter how hard he tried.

Then J. Dan eventing, the strings of ritual moving his hands, arms, legs, and mouth.

VECTORS OF SUNLIGHT CONTRA THE CIRCULAR MOTIF.

J. Dan turns around in his sleep, and lumbers slowly toward him in a cumbrous cowboy's dance, and Laurel is suddenly there too, crying, and the three of them embrace and say yes, and then Jeffrey is once more asleep, dreaming.